Dolly Lloyd is a Moldovan-born fashion designer who discovered her passion for fashion at the tender age of six, when her grandmother introduced her to sewing. Post attending school, she completed a degree in fashion at Northumbria University. Having honed her design skills working for various fashion brands, she finally created her own eponymous label under the name Teo Lloyd and opened a prestigious high street boutique in London. Her in-depth knowledge of the industry and insight into luxury brands has inspired her first novel in a forthcoming series.

To Holly

Dream Big

Dennis, Cristian and David, your unconditional love is the tapestry of my creativity, inspiration, and imagination. Your encouragement and support will remain the light and main guidance to everything that I have achieved so far in my life. I can never express enough gratitude and love that I have for you all.

Dolly Lloyd

OLIVIA TAYLOR
FASHION DREAMS

AUSTIN MACAULEY PUBLISHERS™

LONDON • CAMBRIDGE • NEW YORK • SHARJAH

A CIP catalogue record for this title is available from the British Library.

ISBN 9781398448612 (Paperback)
ISBN 9781398448629 (ePub e-book)

www.austinmacauley.com

First Published 2022
Austin Macauley Publishers Ltd®
1 Canada Square
Canary Wharf
London
E14 5AA

Table of Contents

Chapter One
Best Things
Happen Unexpectedly

Olivia stopped for a second before entering a grand, magnificent building with one of the most glamorous, fascinating entrances she had ever seen. Everything around was so polished, luxurious and perfectly placed that it seemed like a fairy-tale. Olivia wore a beautiful white dress and had in her hands a stunning electric blue evening bag. Every little detail seemed to, somehow, match the grand entrance, including the car she had just left.

She had the curious feeling that this was to be one of the most special and important days of her life. People around her smiled as they rushed to put the finishing touches to this magical place. Olivia walked through large, gaping double doors, where a beautiful staircase stood. Moving onto the steps, she immediately remembered that she needed to make a wish – a happy wish that would follow her throughout her life like a shadow. She was ready to close her eyes when, suddenly, everything around her started to vanish. Olivia screamed, unable to feel the stairs under her feet. Her optimism disappeared with them and she felt lost and horrified.

Her eyes snapped open and she sighed in confusion. It took Olivia a little while until she woke properly, pondering what the dream meant – why so beautiful, yet scary at the same time?

In her mid-30s, Olivia was a British girl with natural beauty and a warm, strong character with a great sense of humour and a balanced approach to life. A brunette about 5ft 6in tall, she had a habit of changing her appearance, which reflected the creative side of her personality.

A hard worker, who was career and goal orientated, she was loyal to her friends and took pride in always giving advice from the heart. She wanted the best for herself and the people she liked and loved and never took no for an answer, exploring every avenue to reach her goal and always aiming for perfection. There was a sceptical side to her character too, which she used to her advantage whenever she came across chancers looking to take advantage of her, though, thankfully, there had been very few of them.

Olivia loved her Surrey country home, which was her favourite place in the world, where she loved to escape. Sitting down in her living room, she looked through large Victorian windows at her garden. The view was so beautiful. A winding path cut through a stunning landscape containing beds of vibrant, colourful flowers with ferns cut into witches' hats, orange and red acers, cherry trees and other foliage.

Lying beneath the window was Duke, her loving dog, enjoying the sun. It was a beautiful sunny day and Olivia felt wrapped up in the mystical nature of her dream, focusing on its finer moments when she felt like a princess. It was a perfect picture and she wanted to stop time and make the moment last as long as possible.

The phone rang, distracting her from her cosy little place. She looked at the phone to see who was calling but failed to recognise the number. Olivia never answered her phone if she didn't know who it was, but, surprisingly, on this occasion, she did so without hesitation.

"Hello, may I speak to Miss Taylor, please?"

"Yes, speaking," said Olivia.

"My name is Derek Smart and I work in the recruitment department of The Delaney Brothers."

Olivia became a little nervous. She wasn't prepared for a conversation like this but excitement mingled with her nerves, lending her the courage to respond. "Hello, Derek," she said as calmly as she could manage. "I applied for a position within your company."

"That's right, Miss Taylor. You didn't receive our subsequent email?"

"I didn't, no."

"It must have ended up in your junk mailbox," said Derek. "Please, take a look and if you're still interested, let us know."

Still interested? Thought Olivia. That sounded promising. "I'll go and check in a moment and will get back to you later on today. Thanks so much for your call."

"No problem. I look forward to your response."

They exchanged pleasantries to end the call and Olivia went straight to her computer to check her spam mail. Sure enough, Derek's email awaited her, wrongly deposited in her junk folder. She waited a few moments; her hands starting to shake through nerves. It was a peculiar feeling and she worried that she'd somehow misinterpreted his call or that

11

she'd slipped into another dream. Opening Derek's email, she began to read…

Dear, Miss Olivia Spencer Taylor,

Thank you for the interest you showed in our company. We have carefully evaluated your application and CV and taking into account your broad knowledge and experience in high end fashion and luxury, we are delighted to offer you the position of creative director in our company.

As a highly prestigious fashion house, our company needs innovative styles and fresh ideas and we believe you are the best candidate for the position. Your style in design is very much in line with our brand and we believe your natural gifts can enhance our identity to help us become even more exclusive and chic.

We will negotiate salary and benefits once you confirm interest in taking the offered position. We will also send you a contract detailing our employment practices, including benefits and entitlements, such as performance-related bonuses, annual leave and all other relevant information. We look forward to your response and hope to welcome you to The Delaney Brothers family! With best wishes,

Derek Smart.

Olivia smiled broadly but managed to suppress a yelp of excitement. The email she had just received was a dream for all aspiring designers, who would die to work for one of the world's most famous fashion houses.

She stopped for a second, thinking how lucky she was. She had only sent the application a week ago but had been offered the position of her dreams via phone, without even having an interview. She tempered her excitement with a fat dose of realism. Big companies made their selections from a huge array of candidates and employed head-hunters to find the most suitable people. Knowing that it would be foolish to respond immediately to Derek's email, her best friend, Andrew, popped into her head. Great at giving advice, Olivia realised she had to see him to receive his counsel.

Andrew had been Olivia's friend since they had been at university around 13 years earlier. Having met at a friend's party, their bond had been solid and they were pretty much inseparable. Andrew was a tall handsome man, who always attracted attention no matter where he went, but his main trait was his captivating character. He was a real old school gentleman and Olivia always went to him for advice. And, at 46 years old, he had knowledge and intelligence in abundance.

Olivia had a crush on him from the very beginning but with Andrew being in a long-term relationship with a lovely girl called Hannah, she swapped any romantic aspirations for a warm, balanced friendship. The fact that Olivia and Hannah became such good friends killed any possibility that she and Andrew might one day come together.

Olivia called Andrew but as he failed to answer, she decided to leave him a voicemail message, asking him to reply ASAP. She went and made herself a tea and decided to take a walk in the garden with Duke. Needing a distraction until she spoke to Andrew, Olivia sat down on a bench and closed her eyes.

Sensing that a short meditation would do her good, with her mind overwhelmed by the job offer, she spent a while calming her thoughts. Duke played his part in helping to redirect her thinking by running around her and pestering her to play his favourite game of catch a ball. In no time, Olivia felt totally relaxed and free of stress. *Dogs always manage to make us feel great,* she thought.

Walking back into the house, Olivia remembered that she had a yoga class to attend and that she couldn't cancel because she had promised her friend, Evelin, she would go.

At the gym, Olivia met her two female best friends, Anna and Evelin. Having been mates since college, they called themselves 'The A Team'. Thirty-three years old, Evelin was a tall and beautiful girl with ginger hair and big blue eyes. Her personality was the opposite of Olivia's, with calmness and balance the main traits of her character. She was hard to read sometimes but happy and fulfilled. Anna, on the other hand, was a sexy blonde with curves. Aged 36, she had a great sense of humour and was a little on the wild side; very fitness orientated but never quite fulfilling her goals.

Olivia was so happy to see the pair and after an hour of intense yoga, they headed to the local coffee shop.

"This is my favourite café," mentioned Evelin, who went straight to her regular spot to sit down. "Girls, just for the record, if you can't ever get hold of me, you know where to find me – right here!"

Anna looked at her and smiled. "We always have great giggles and must make more of an effort to see each other more often. What about you, Olivia? You look quiet today."

"I don't know where to start," said Olivia. "I've had a rather interesting day. I've been offered a job and even got chased for an answer. You both know I've been looking for a new job in fashion, don't you? Well, to cut a long story short,

I received a call from The Delaney Brothers. I've been offered the position of creative director, with no interview involved. Does this sound real to you?"

Both girls looked shocked, speaking at the same time as if in one voice, "Are you serious?"

"Yes, I am," continued Olivia. "And I can't get hold of Andrew – he isn't answering the phone when I need him most."

"Don't worry about Andrew – he'll call you back," said Anna. "Is there anything we can do to help you?"

"Yes – find Andrew and bring him to me!" said Olivia with a smile.

The girls looked at each other and giggled.

"Yes, your guardian angel is lost – what a disaster!" joked Anna.

"Are you going to accept the job?" asked Evelin. "It might sound strange to other people but not to us. You're a very talented person with a huge portfolio for your young age. You have broad experience working for luxury fashion houses and brands. Since you graduated several years ago, you've accumulated amazing knowledge and not one of the companies you worked for wanted to let you go. You left because you felt unfulfilled and wanted more from your career. You'll be a great asset to them and they'll love you and your talent."

"Okay, my cheeks are burning," murmured an embarrassed but grateful Olivia. "I think that's enough for now, girls. I'm definitely going to accept the position. Let's face it; it's a dream come true. I just need to reply to them and confirm that I'm interested. This is a great opportunity for me, going back to where I belong – in fashion."

Evelin and Anna leaned in towards Olivia to give her a huge girly hug.

"We're here for you no matter what," Anna began. "It's great to know you'll start a new chapter in your beloved world of fashion. But when you become famous, don't forget about us! We're your partners in crime – for better and worse!"

Olivia felt so happy and secure next to her friends and considered how fortunate she was to have them in her life. Her phone rang…and guess who was calling? – Andrew! The girls looked at each other and made funny faces.

"Hello, Andrew!" Olivia answered chirpily.

"Hi, Olivia," said Andrew. "I'm sorry for missing your call."

"That's fine," said Olivia. "I'm with Anna and Evelin at the moment, having a coffee at our favourite café. Would you like to join us?"

"Why not? I'm only around the corner. See you in a bit."

"He's on his way to join us." Olivia smiled once their conversation had ended. "Shall we grab something to eat before Andrew shows up? Something light and healthy like a quinoa salad, maybe? After all, we're the health queens!"

While the girls were eating their salads, Andrew entered the premises.

Anna was the first to break the silence. "Now, that is a total transformation, Andrew – the new hairstyle really suits you!"

"Yes, it does," Evelin confirmed. "What a change!"

A bashful Andrew looked at the girls and blushed, scraping his fringe back from his forehead. "Thank you, girls," he said, sitting down and ordering a coffee and a sandwich. "It's nice to see you all again. This is something that I've been missing; a casual catch-up."

"Yes, you're right but, frankly, we have to leave soon," said Anna. "Why don't we get together one evening and have a nice time like we always do?"

"That's a great idea!" Olivia, Andrew and Evelin confirmed in one voice.

"So, what's going on?" asked Andrew, turning to Olivia. "What was so important for you to want to meet up?"

"Oh, it's a coincidence," confirmed Olivia. "We have a yoga class together every week at the same time and you called back while we were having a little catch-up."

"What was it you wanted to ask me?" Andrew enquired.

"Well, I've received a job offer from The Delaney Brothers and I need your opinion."

"A job offer from The Delaney Brothers? Wow!" Smiled Andrew. "Congratulations! What a nice surprise. Only two days ago, you were complaining that you needed a job and now you have this fantastic opportunity."

"Yes," said Olivia. "That's what I'm afraid of. This whole situation sounds unreal. I promised to reply to them today but I'm a little overwhelmed!"

"Do you have your tablet or laptop with you, so that we can have a look at the email?" asked Andrew.

While Olivia opened her tablet to connect to the internet, Evelin and Anna announced that they were leaving and that a date in the diary had to be placed for the evening out. They all agreed and the girls gave Andrew and Olivia a hug, blowing a kiss on the way out.

"Okay, now I can read the email," said Andrew once Olivia had handed him her tablet.

After a minute or so of silence, Andrew looked up and smiled. "This is an amazing opportunity and I'm convinced you'll have a nice salary and overall package. You mentioned that you had a phone call from them as well. Did that happen today?"

"Yes," Olivia answered. "I got the call early this morning. I was very surprised and didn't engage very much but have promised to look at the email and reply with an answer. Their original email ended up in my spam folder."

Andrew gently placed his hand on Olivia's shoulder. "Since the first day I met you, your passion, hobby, devotion and life in general have been about fashion. You love your creative world and this whole situation sounds great. Having known you for so long, nothing really surprises me. You're the most positive, hardworking woman I've ever known. You deserve this. In my opinion, they offered you the position immediately because of your experience, knowledge, talent and style in design. Everything is in your portfolio and CV. You have nothing to lose. In fact, you'll gain a lot of experience and I can feel that this is the beginning of something great happening in your life. Opportunities like that only happen to great, hardworking people like you!"

Olivia had looked like a little girl with an innocent face in need of reassurance but Andrew's words inspired her. She gave him a huge hug. "Thank you for being there for me. I'll email them to confirm the position. I'm ready for a new chapter in my life – a great fashion challenge!" Hannah popped into her head. "I haven't even asked how you and Hannah are. I saw those pictures of your fabulous holiday in Mykonos on social media."

"We're well, thank you." Smiled Andrew. "I can't really complain. Mykonos was such a great place. I can definitely recommend it – not only is it beautiful but fashion-orientated as well. Everybody looks like they should be on a magazine cover. Maybe it could be your next holiday destination?"

He checked his watch. "Sorry, but I have to leave now because the rest of my day is really busy. I'm working from home today and am meeting Hannah for a drink when she arrives at the station. You can join us if you want?"

"I can't but thank you," said Olivia. "I have to go home and focus on the email I'm going to be sending to The Delaney Brothers. Have a nice evening and lots of love to Hannah from me. By the way, your haircut's a winner – a nice change."

"It's great to know that it's been approved by you all!" Laughed Andrew.

He stood up, kissed Olivia on the cheek and waved goodbye before leaving the premises. Olivia sat on her own for a while, looking at her iPad and reading the new emails she had just received. Her mind was entirely focused on how best she could construct her email but after a few minutes, she decided to return home. It was already midday and she had to fire it off by the day's end. *At home, I would be able to relax enough to put the perfect response together,* she thought as she readied herself to leave.

Olivia had such a disciplined life that even when she didn't work, she was totally organised and almost every hour was accounted for in her diary. Before driving back home, she made a few phone calls and cancelled whatever she had booked for the rest of the day. On the way back, she popped into her local supermarket to buy some chicken treats for Duke and some ingredients for her evening meal.

When she got home, she gave her loving Duke a huge hug and kissed him, then made a nice cup of tea and sat down to finally reply to the email.

Chapter Two
We Get in Life What We
Have the Courage to Ask For

Olivia rushed through the house in search of her umbrella. The British weather was so unpredictable, at the best of times that it made sense to have some protection in case it rained – especially as she had spent so long readying herself for such an important day.

She sat down for a moment to think. *This is your dream job, Olivia, and being nervous doesn't help*, she told herself. Realising that it was better to leave the house than sit there procrastinating and risk being late for her first day of work, she left the house.

She decided to drive to work in case the train got delayed. It was such an important day and knowing how significant first impressions were, she called on the disciplined side of her personality, which always targeted perfection. Within a minute or two, she was sat behind the wheel of her ocean-blue Niro, self-charging hybrid electric car. She started the engine and having selected some nice chill out music on the car stereo, began her journey into London.

While Olivia's focus was on the road, amid the busy early morning traffic, the butterflies in her stomach kept her excited and the music in the car balanced her feelings. Today was a day that she had been very much looking forward to, having closed her company down six months before. A luxury fashion company, she had been unable to find the funding required to maintain it long enough for it to make serious waves in the industry, despite manifold compliments as to the quality of the clothes in its name.

It would have taken a good five years to make a profit and, sadly, Olivia had been unable to source the funding required to maintain the business that long. While disappointed that things hadn't gone according to plan, she saw it as a valuable life lesson and had moved on with positive energy and fire in her belly to really make her mark in the industry and hoped to create her own brand in the future.

Olivia's favourite inspirational quote was *"Failure is an illusion";* something she related to. While nobody deliberately set out to flop, she realised that 'failure' was in fact an invitation to gain priceless knowledge, experience and confidence. Her close friends always claimed that she should become an inspirational coach and encourage everybody to get out there and never give up. And if things didn't work out, she believed, then new avenues should be explored.

Uplifted by a fantastically positive vibe, Olivia arrived in London and stopped in front of the building, which would now be her place of work. It was a tall, modern structure, almost entirely made of glass with a beautiful entrance and seemingly endless space in its lobby.

The underground car park was easy to follow and had plenty of parking spaces. After parking up, Olivia left the car park and walked through the lobby. Reaching reception, a young Asian woman sat behind a desk, smiling warmly. Olivia could see from her name tag that she was called Asha.

"Good morning," she said brightly.

"Good morning," Olivia replied. "My name is Olivia Taylor and I'm here to start work."

"Oh, yes, hi, Olivia," said Asha, handing her, her ID. "Here's your ID, which will give you access to the building. Your office is on the fourth floor. The meeting room is on the same floor, which you should find handy. A weekly meeting starts at nine prompt every Monday morning, so please make your way, there in enough time."

"Thank you, I will." Smiled Olivia, setting off for the elevator, which was positioned at the far end of the lobby. Before stepping inside, she took a few moments to glance around. She felt so happy, having always loved beautiful things and nice places…and now she would be spending a minimum of five days a week in such a great environment.

In the elevator, she met two of her work colleagues, Stephanie and Mark. Tall and beautiful, Stephanie looked like an editorial model. She wore oversized blouse and skinny leather trousers, and Olivia felt that she could read her personality from her style – she was a fun girl; a fashion rock star. Mark, on the other hand, looked like a perfect country magazine model with smart jeans, a v neck jumper and casual blazer. They both worked in the marketing department and offered Olivia help if she got stuck with anything at the beginning of her tenure.

Olivia waved, thanking them for being helpful before leaving the elevator. It was only then that she realised she was on the wrong floor, so decided to take the stairs to the next floor up. As she was about to open the door to the Design Department, she heard voices, pausing to listen.

"It'll be interesting to see what our new creative director looks like – a librarian or fashionista?"

"I hope she'll be nice to us. I can't believe you haven't googled her – you can see her on social media."

Oh well, thought Olivia. *This is the fashion world after all, which guarantees a mix of personalities.*

She opened the door and surprised the mean-talking girls, who had been looking at the elevator rather than the door leading to the stairs, expecting her to step out of the former. As soon as they saw her, they dispersed, Olivia assuming they thought they had been overheard. They were right, she acknowledged amusedly. Welcome to the fashion world!

She found her cosy new office, which had her name on its door and stepped inside to find a beautiful bouquet of flowers sitting in an ornate vase. Looking at the accompanying card, it came as no surprise to find that Andrew, Evelin and Anna had sent them. After taking a quick look through the window, Olivia checked the time. Coming up to 9 am, she took a deep breath and made for the meeting room.

Entering, it was a spacious room containing a long beige table, around which her fellow staff members sat in reclining black leather chairs.

"Good morning, Olivia!" Smiled the Managing Director, Sarah.

In her late 50s, she had a classic look and the kind of demeanour that immediately led Olivia to believe she didn't suffer fools gladly. She looked completely at ease with her surroundings as if she had been there a long while.

"Hello, yes. I'm very pleased to meet you."

24

"And you," Sarah replied, stepping towards and hugging Olivia. She turned to address the other people gathered. "As you all know, Olivia is our new creative director, who I know you'll make her feel as welcome as possible."

Hmmm, thought Olivia, recalling the women from a few minutes earlier.

While her other colleagues introduced themselves, offering help and guidance, she noticed an impeccably dressed man who said very little, keeping himself to himself. Olivia considered that he may have been more reserved than most and needed more time to reveal his true personality.

The meeting was relatively short and was essentially a goal-setting, motivational affair that set everybody up for the week ahead. Overall, Olivia was very happy meeting everybody and felt welcome and safe. Despite the company being large and global, the London office felt like a family.

After the meeting, she introduced herself to everybody in her department, which was around 20-people strong. She wanted to ensure that everybody was engaged and listening to what she had to say. Olivia had a nice considerate character, who took time to speak to everybody and remember their names. She was a great team player – something they would soon be aware of – but hoped that nobody would underestimate her. That was when things could go very wrong, for she could also be stubborn and disciplined, as well as charming and patient.

A few minutes after taking a seat in her office, she heard a knock on the door.

"Come in," she said, raising her voice a touch.

In walked the two young women from earlier.

"Hi," said one of them. A pretty redhead with a fantastic figure, she had a lovely little dimple smile and was mixed race. "I'm Madeline and I wanted to apologise for earlier. I, um…well…we were just having a chat among ourselves and didn't mean any harm."

"Yes," the other woman echoed. She had lovely clear skin and long blonde tresses. "No harm or offence intended."

"And none taken." Smiled Olivia. "Curiosity is a gift that all we creatives possess. And I'm not Cruella de Vil! Can you please explain your position within the company?"

"Gladly," said the blonde lady. "I'm Samantha and I'm an embroidery designer. I've been here from almost six years and I sign off all of the company's embroidery designs."

"And I'm a junior designer," said Madeline. "I've been here nearly two years and love being a part of what we're doing here."

"Those are both very impressive, important jobs and I'm very much looking forward to working with you. Let's forget what happened earlier and make a fresh start. It's been lovely meeting you." Olivia offered her hand to both of them and felt relieved when their palms touched, amid friendly smiles.

Olivia spent the whole afternoon arranging her schedule for preparation of the firm's new collection. It was her first collection with the company and she needed to make sure everything was by the book, starting with its brand identity and including deadlines and the perfect fashion show, which had to grab the attention of the catwalk-covering press. Fashion was an industry in which pressure was an integral part of any project but pressure, to Olivia, was part of what drove her. *For the next week, I'll have to work on the inspiration and mood board,* she thought. *This has to be one of the best collections The Delaney Brothers has ever seen.*

Olivia's first day at work whizzed by and before she knew it, she was on her way to meet Anna at the Savoy cocktail bar, having arranged to meet a couple of days earlier. Typically busy and welcoming, Olivia approached the bar. She was surprised to find Anna talking to a very handsome man as she was already seeing somebody. The moment she approached them, Anna introduced Olivia to her cousin, Dominic, who looked around the late 20s / early 30s mark.

"Congratulations on your first day in your new job," he said a little bashfully. "Anna has been telling me all about you. Anyway, I'd better leave you ladies to it. Have fun and I'll see you later."

"Bye, Dom." Smiled Anna.

"Where have you been hiding your cousin?" asked Olivia. "He's very handsome!"

"He's too young for you!" joked Anna. "He's only 24!"

"Are you for real? He could easily be in his 30s! Whatever – his age doesn't change the fact that he's smoking hot!"

She ordered a bottle of champagne from a suave-looking waiter wearing a crisp, immaculate white jacket, paying him and sipping from her glass.

"I can't believe you fancy my cousin!" Anna laughed. "Now that you're working again, you're noticing men again. I figure you're taking things step-by-step – career first, then a man."

The girls looked at each other and giggled.

"I miss your funny, cheeky jokes, Anna," said Olivia. "Now that we're both working in the same part of London,

27

we can have more drinks and dinners. We can even drag Evelin along to our little after-work affairs!"

"Sounds great! I hope that we can change Evelin's family habits. She's such a great wife and mum but not so great with friends anymore."

"Well, this is our challenge then," suggested Olivia. "But first, tell me how you are?"

"I don't know where to start." Sighed Anna. "I'm still seeing Aron but I know I need to stop. It's not really working. The sex is great but that's about all there is to it for me. Plus, while I'm seeing him, it stops me seeing anybody else. Maybe now that I can meet you more often in town, I can change my habits and start to sort my life out."

"Yes, of course," Olivia said. "I'm totally yours if you need any advice or help." They sat and talked for a good few hours after that. It was a nice, relaxed evening and they both needed it in order to catch-up.

Olivia arrived home a few hours later and after a nice bath, went to bed, feeling satisfied with her first day at The Delaney Brothers, yet still a little overwhelmed by it. She tried to sleep but her mind was too alert, so she got out of bed and went downstairs into the kitchen. Opening the fridge, she grabbed a bottle of champagne, the only alcoholic drink she liked and poured herself a glass.

Sitting in front of the television, she noticed that it was nearly midnight. Not willing to waste any time, she set about scribbling her thoughts down and creating a schedule for the busy week ahead. She was aware that she could easily become a workaholic but fashion was in her blood and she was determined to create a good impression with her new employer.

For the next few days, Olivia gathered tonnes of information that would help her create an inspiration board. She focused on the company's brand signature, style and designs and was working closely with two in-house designers when her office door opened and in walked Baptiste, one of the main designers who she met on the first day when Sarah introduced her to everybody. She had noticed then that he was very reserved and didn't really make an effort to say hi properly. Like then, he was immaculately dressed and the arrogance she had perceived was demonstrated when he asked sarcastically in his French accent, "How come I'm not involved in the up-and-coming collection? I've been with the company for over 11 years and know what works best and what we should do to make it even better."

"Why don't you join us?" asked Olivia in a calm voice. "It was never my intention to exclude you from the team. How fabulous to know that you've been with the company for that long. Your experience and opinions will definitely be valuable to all of us here. My apologies if I've offended you in any way. You've been a little reserved, so I thought you might need more time to get to know me."

Baptiste sat down with them and helped contribute to the group session, though their exchange made Olivia aware that he might have been a little jealous of her and that she needed to find a way to get to know him.

Time flies when you love what you do, Olivia thought to herself. Her first week at work was almost over and she was entirely satisfied with what she had achieved so far. It was late afternoon on a Friday and she still had a lot of work to complete. She hadn't planned to leave the premises until her project for the week was complete and accepted she might have to put some additional hours in the following day in order to finalise the inspiration board for the new collection.

She was excited at how well the collection was shaping up and looked at the wall in front of her, which was transformed into a huge board with different shapes and structured lines on one side and colours and countless images on the other.

Olivia was such an old-fashioned girl when it came to creating a collection. She preferred to research, print everything out and then cut out the most important images, which would come alive on her board. The digital world was fascinating to her and once she had her board finalised, she would have it translated digitally.

Creating an inspirational board was the embryo of the collection and it had to be right in order to execute the next step. It was like the beginning of a puzzle that eventually got completed. As far as she was concerned, designers were special creatives. Inspiration came from many different avenues and total chaos ensued when they didn't know when to stop. Once a designer was in a creative mood and in harmony with what he or she was doing, new great inventions were born.

Luxury and couture brands were fashion's driving force with trends, colours, styles and fabrics, all invented via collaboration by the globe's amazing designers; the geniuses behind the fashion world.

Olivia replaced some of the images on the board and cut out some more to add to it but something was missing and she was determined to find the final piece of the puzzle. Hearing a knock on the door, Olivia put her pencil down.

"Come in."

Her assistant, Michael, entered the room. Tall and barrel-chested, he wore skinny trousers and a purple silk shirt; his dark beard, a different shade to his mousey coloured hair.

"Is there anything to do before the end of the day?" he asked with a friendly smile.

"No." Olivia smiled back at him. "Thank you for the effort and work you've put in throughout the week and have a great weekend."

"And you," said Michael before leaving.

Olivia continued looking at the board. In her mind, she was already designing and could clearly see some of the lines from the board implemented on a dress or a long skirt. Finding her pencil, she started to draw. It wasn't long after that she approached the board and started to remove some images from one side of it. A beaming smile appeared on her face. She had finally found the missing piece from the board. She knew exactly what it was and where it should go…but with the cleaning lady, switching her vacuum cleaner on, she felt distracted.

Olivia went to the kitchen and made a cup of tea. On the kitchen table, virtually begging her to take a bite, was a lemon cake. When it came to sweets, Olivia just went for it, only thinking about the consequences later or maybe not at all. She took a slice and started nibbling at it…and, hell, did it taste good.

While taking a break, she decided to look at her personal emails and messages. She had been very busy recently and hadn't really kept in touch with anybody other than seeing Anna for an evening, so decided to text her friends to keep them updated as to her new life venture. So involved in this

31

was she that she failed to realise she was already onto her second slice of cake and that the vacuuming had stopped.

Olivia took her tea back to her office and sat down, looking at the board. It was late evening and amazingly quiet – the perfect atmosphere for creative endeavours. She was tempted to stay even longer but remembered that poor Duke had been waiting for her all day. Having somebody help her by feeding him and taking him out for walks made her neglect him a little. A wave of guilt washed over her but her work was so important and kept her so busy that sacrifices needed to be made – in the short-term, at least until she had fully adapted to her new role. Glancing once more at the board, Olivia left her office.

Chapter Three
Great Success Is Achieved
Only via Teamwork

The great career adventure that Olivia embarked on a few months before, started to show its results. She felt that she had been destined for the role of creative director, given her leadership qualities and the way in which she worked with her team. Most of the required fabrics had been selected from various fashion shows all over the world, while the designers working under her were busy putting the finishing touches to the collection drawings.

Olivia sat in her office with a cornucopia of designs spread all over the floor and on the board. To finalise a collection of drawings was almost an art in itself but before she decided to invite her team to help her, she needed to cast her eye over all of the designs and remove any that failed to stand out or which looked too similar to others while retaining those she thought would work great on samples.

Several days had already been accounted for, working on the collection and adapting all of the detailed designs to the drawings. Finally looking satisfied, she figured it was time to invite her team of designers, who had worked closely with her to have a little fun finalising the drawing capsules.

Samantha, Madeline, George and Baptiste entered the meeting room, which was set up with a huge screen and several boards. They all looked excited other than Baptiste, who had retained a distant, serious attitude.

A lively young man of Spanish origin, who had a colourful personality, George broke the silence. "Thank you for inviting all of us to finalise the drawing designs. This is my first experience of it as our previous creative director preferred to finalise the drawings by himself. He only briefed us about what was needed and how we had to deliver it. He was very kind to us but preferred to work individually."

"Well, we're all very different in our approach," said Olivia with a smile. "Personally, I prefer working with my team. You've all put in huge amounts of effort to get to this stage and you all deserve to have an input in finalising the drawings." She looked at the screen. "Let's get started, shall we? I've organised the screen because I think it's easier to choose the drawings from a big screen and with the technology so advanced, we can create a digital board now."

"Good idea," said Samantha as everybody sat down.

Baptiste sat at the end of the table, and looked to be deliberately distancing himself from the rest of the team. He looked at Olivia and said: "I don't know what you want us to do. From my experience, this can turn out to be a mess. We all have different opinions and styles, don't we?"

"Yes, we do," said Olivia. "But this is a great opportunity to learn how to adapt and how to take other ideas on board. We're all adults and we all want to achieve something special and unique this season. I'm sure you'll enjoy the experience. Don't you think?"

Baptiste blushed a little and said nothing in return. *Why is this guy so stubborn, arrogant and opinionated?* Olivia asked herself. *He needs to relax and start to get to know me – I'm not his enemy!* But she didn't have time to think about Baptiste at that moment, so she asked each designer to look at the pile of drawings on the table and point out those that they believed would have a stronger, innovative impact on the collection. After that, they could start to add them to the digital board and see how the drawings connected with each other.

Olivia sat down next to them and started to look through the pile of drawings that she had already condensed a few days ago. They were quickly separated by the team and, in no time, the digital board started to come alive and the drawings looked amazing. Olivia looked radiant and satisfied, thinking to herself, *Moments like this should never be forgotten!* After a few hours of intense work, everybody in the room was happy with the result – even Baptiste looked happier and more engaged.

With the designs for the collection finalised, Olivia felt the need to see her friends and relax a little before the sample process began. Samples were the most important part of the process, embodying the end product that would be shown on the catwalks. So this was the only window for her to see her dear friends and relax a little.

Olivia picked her phone up and dialled Evelin's number. She knew that Evelin was always busy with her family but planned to drag her into town and make sure she got to have a little fun outside of her comfort zone.

Evelin answered the phone singing a lullaby to her four-year-old daughter, Francis. Olivia almost thought it was for her and was ready to start telling her off when Evelin just softly sang, "Please, help me, I need a break!"

Olivia giggled and said, "We definitely have telepathic connections! I was calling you to ask if you can come out on Friday."

"Like attracts like and I'm so happy to hear your voice," Evelin continued.

"I'll call you in 30 minutes," she sang before putting the phone down.

Olivia smiled and thought, *I'm not ready for a family – and that's a fact!* She valued her freedom too much for that type of commitment and loved her life as it was. But she also loved children and definitely wanted a family one day.

Grabbing her handbag and some folders, she headed for the elevator as it was time for her to go home. As she was driving when Evelin called her back, she pulled over and kept the engine running, singing to her friend, "Hello, crazy mama! I hope Francis hasn't asked you what was that all about?"

Evelin laughed and said, "You're absolutely right. The moment I hung up, she asked me, "Did you sing that to me or Auntie Olivia?" So I told her that Auntie Olivia sometimes needed a lullaby too." They both laughed.

Evelin continued, "What is this night out about? Is it anything special?"

"No, but we can make it special," said Olivia. "We're the experts at it!"

"Yes, I'm definitely coming," said Evelin. "Who else will be there?"

"Guess what – I called you first as I know you need a little relaxing time. And besides, I know Anna will come with us no matter what – she's our party buddy!"

"Yes, you're right," said Evelin. "What about Andrew?"

"Of course – ask him as well," said Olivia. "It'll be good to see you all again. I have some invitations to a lounge party. We can have dinner, then go to the party. We need to eat because I know we'll end up having a lot to drink!"

Evelin laughed again. "Leave it with me. I'll call Anna and Andrew and help to organise the restaurant."

"See you on Friday," they sang to each other.

Olivia felt happy, knowing that Evelin was looking forward to their meet-up and upon arriving home, she took a bath and went straight to bed afterwards. As she drifted off, she smiled, pleased with what had been a long but productive day…and safe in the knowledge that a good night's sleep would help her feel totally recharged in the morning.

The next day, as she had expected, Olivia felt ready to conquer the world. Her mind was alive with fresh, new ideas and she was determined to get to work as soon as possible. Shortly after arriving at The Delaney Brothers, she asked Michael to join her in her office.

"Here," she said, handing him a document, containing various tasks. "I usually send you an email but today is an important day as we're starting to develop and create the samples. I'll be out of the office for most of the day but want to make sure everything is going according to the plan we made, please keep me updated as you go. We don't have time to waste."

"Don't worry," Michael tried to reassure her. "Everything will be done before lunch and if anything changes, I'll let you know."

Olivia grinned with relief. She was pleased with Michael, who was quick, efficient and easy going – a great colleague to work with. She had two meetings that day but it was hugely reassuring to know that by the time she returned to her office, everything would be done. She really had a fantastic team under her, all of whom worked hard to achieve great results.

With it being a Friday, Olivia remembered that she needed to double check if the party that she was invited to was still on and that her friends had been added to the guest list. With her excitement growing about her evening out, she rushed out of the building and hailed a taxi to take her to her meetings.

Meetings in town were always tricky with heavy traffic, the main obstacle, so leaving early was always a bonus. The company had a production office a few miles away and Olivia took the time to look once more through the folder in her hand. She was meeting the pattern-cutting and seamstress team, which would create the end product, the samples. They tested the collection's essential components and it couldn't be clearer that Silvia, the head seamstress, was a hugely talented lady. Seemingly quiet and reserved by nature, she was amazingly sharp when it came to business. A petit lady in her 50s, Silvia had short dark hair and was raised in Italy.

"Hello, everybody!" Olivia said upon entering the atelier, where Silvia and her team awaited her.

As far as Olivia was concerned, the atelier was the heart of the brand. A huge room, it contained rows of sewing machines, mannequins, fabrics and patterns. For the most part, highly skilled middle-aged ladies manned the machines with a smattering of young interns learning their trade from them.

"Hi!" Silvia's team cried in unison.

"We're so pleased to see you again!" Giggled Silvia.

"Thank you, and I you." Olivia ordered a decaf coffee from one of the interns and sat down. "We're officially starting to create the samples today. I know that we have a lot of tailoring and some draping involved. The collection is pretty structured and elegant with an innovative twist and it demands strict attention to detail – especially in relation to the new details and embroidery."

She thanked the intern for her coffee, took a sip and then continued, "You all impressed me with your talent when we tested the new detail designs a couple of weeks ago. We'll go over the design specifications today and I'll visit the atelier on a daily basis. This is one of my favourite parts of the development when reality meets fantasy and creates a bond to deliver the identity of the new collection. Please, make sure that any problems are reported to me directly, so that we can try and solve them as soon as possible."

After several hours going over the design specifications, Olivia left the atelier with a huge smile on her face. She knew that the team, she left behind there, would deliver the impossible if they had to. Sid, the main pattern cutter, was such a special man, who had been working in the company for 23 years and whose talent and ambition had gained renown even outside of the company. With Silvia and Sid on her side, Olivia felt secure and confident that the samples would start to come to life even earlier then she expected. *There's nothing better in life then a great team*, she thought.

It was Friday lunch time and Olivia was still in her office with plenty of work yet to be done. Michael entered the office and reminded her that she had a hair appointment in 20 minutes. So busy had she been that it was only then that she remembered that today was the day when she would be heading out on the town with her close friends.

Olivia rushed to the appointment, not liking to be late and reached the hair salon just in time. Kate, one of the main stylists, welcomed her. In her late 20s, she had a natural beauty that required little make-up, her dark brown tresses tumbling over her shoulders.

"Hi, Olivia! I haven't seen you for a few weeks. But you look radiant and happy, I must say."

Olivia smiled back at her. "I haven't seen my close friends for a while due to my busy schedule but today we're finally getting together. So that must be behind my radiant look! Let's have a little fun with my hair as well – maybe something more glam with volume."

"Sounds great," said Kate, handing Olivia some fashion magazines to flick through. "I have to ask how's the collection going?"

"Everything is great and the collection is something special to me. We're on schedule and all of my team are very talented individuals. That really helps and is the only way to achieve great results."

Towards the end of her appointment, when her hair was almost done, a lady entered the salon with her young daughter. The little girl was beautiful and Olivia was fixated looking at her. The girl rushed through the salon and stopped in front of her.

"I like your dress." She smiled shyly. "It's beautiful and is my favourite colour."

Initially speechless, Olivia looked at the little girl, who looked and sounded like an angel. "Thank you," she said a few moments later. "What a lovely compliment from a beautiful princess like you!"

"When I grow up, I want to make dresses like yours," the little girl continued.

Olivia leaned closer to her. "If you love it so much, then make it your dream and when you grow up, you can make it real," she said with a wink.

Her mum – a tall, pretty, slender lady – looked at her child, raising her voice a little to say, "Olivia, leave the lady alone – we have to go now." She smiled at Olivia.

"Sorry, madam, she's an inquisitive child."

Olivia sat still for a second like a statue, then smiled at Olivia's mum. "Not at all. In fact, I'm very impressed with her character and charm. She reminds me of myself. I'm called Olivia too, by the way," she said shaking little Olivia's hand.

"Nice to meet you."

They both smiled and winked at each other. The little girl's mum smiled, then left the salon with her daughter.

"What are the chances of meeting a replica of yourself in a little human being?" Olivia asked Kate. "I'm amazed!"

"Yes, that's very rare unless you're blood related," said Kate, who looked as surprised as Olivia by what had just occurred.

"Is her mum a regular at the salon?"

"No, I haven't really seen her before," said Kate.

"Please, can you find out? I'm a little inquisitive."

On her way out, Kate pulled Olivia to one side. "About that lady – she's from a foster charity organisation and left some cards with us – here, take one. She might not even be Olivia's mum."

"Oh, don't say that!" Olivia smiled. "This is getting spooky!" And with that, she left the salon.

The evening approached fast and Olivia left work, looking stunning in a beautiful vine colour dress and black stiletto sandals. Her hair looked sexy on one shoulder and her handbag was a beautiful addition to her look. The whole office kept looking at her as she left and she thought, *well, looks like I'm going to conquer the night*. After catching a cab to the restaurant, they would be kicking their night off at, Olivia entered the premises, heading for the bar, where Andrew was stood. He looked at her, his mouth gaping open.

"Is there anything wrong with me?" she asked. "Everybody's staring at me and I don't know if it's because I've put a great look together or a wrong one."

Andrew inched a little closer to Olivia. "You look beautiful. No wonder you have a lot of eyes on you. I think work has a hugely positive influence on your life. You're radiant and sexy, my dear friend!"

"You're right." Beamed Olivia. "I feel great. I love my job, my friends and my life in general!"

Evelin appeared behind them. "Heh, get a room, you two! I'm feeling left out here!"

Olivia gave them both a huge hug. "Where is Anna, the trouble maker? Is she coming?"

"Of course, she is," said Evelin. "Do you really think you can go out without Anna? We all know that's impossible."

"Yes – you're right!" Laughed Anna, approaching them. "I could hear you from outside talking about me."

"Ah, no – I'm in trouble!" joked Evelin.

They all sat down in a quiet corner of the restaurant. At the next table sat five men, all of whom were looking at them.

Anna turned to Andrew. "I bet they would do anything to replace you, Andrew!"

"Anna, hadn't you better concentrate on our table?" asked Andrew, who looked behind to see what she was talking about.

One of the men – immaculately turned-out with not a hair out of place – stood up and approached their table. "Hi, ladies, sorry to disturb you. I just wanted to say hi to Andrew. We're work colleagues."

"This is Steve, everybody," said Andrew as he stood, shaking his hand. "Steve, have a lovely evening, won't you?"

"And you," said Steve, sitting back down as did Andrew.

"Did he just land from Planet Fit?" Anna asked Andrew. "He's really nice!"

"Ah, no, Anna. He's not your type – far too tidy and trimmed. Your ideal man is the smart, casual Italian stallion type," Olivia said, prompting a bout of laughter.

"It might be but I think I'm getting older and my taste in men is changing," said Anna.

"Look, I'm starving," Evelin grumbled. "Let's eat first, then we can ask Anna what she likes in a man."

"That's a little harsh," said Anna, looking at Evelin. "But you're lucky because I'm starving too!"

"Why don't you order for all of us?" Andrew asked Evelin. "This is our favourite Japanese restaurant and we all have similar tastes."

"Good idea," said Olivia. "Let's share as always."

"I'll order the drinks," Anna began. "If you don't mind. They have a new Sake and it's delicious – you'll all love it."

After everybody had eaten what was, as always, a delicious meal, they all moved to the bar.

"Are you okay?" Olivia asked Andrew, who kept checking his phone. "You look a little distracted."

"Yes, I'm fine. Just going through some messages that Hannah left."

"Why didn't she join us tonight? It would've been great to see her too."

"I agree. I did ask her but she said she already had plans but that she might come to the lounge later on."

"Enough of all that," Anna interrupted. "Tell me more about Steve!"

"I'd better leave you both to talk about Steve," said Olivia. "I'm more interested in a glass of champagne."

While she was ordering the champagne, Evelin stood beside her. "Can you order me a glass too?"

Of course."

"You're a star for thinking of getting all of us together. It's so nice to have a catch-up with you all. I'm a little stuck in Surrey at the moment – the housewife role is not really appealing to me anymore. I'm looking to get a part-time job locally. I'll definitely try to find something in the beauty sector. It's my field of expertise and I love it. I think your work has inspired me to do something with my life too."

"It's only natural that you'll go back to work," said Olivia, who remembered that, prior to having children, Evelin worked as a consultant for a huge beauty and cosmetics company – quite clearly, health and beauty were two factors in her life that she couldn't do without.

"You're an independent, driven woman with an abundance of knowledge and intelligence. Just make sure that your little angels aren't missing you and that you don't go full-time because I know how dedicated and driven you are."

"Yes, for sure," said Evelin. "Family has really changed my priorities but to a large degree, it'll always come first." She raised her glass. "To family and friends!"

Olivia looked at her watch and in a panicked voice said, "We have to leave now, otherwise we won't make it to the party!"

Leaving the restaurant, they piled into Anna's car.

"I can't believe that I'm driving you all tonight," she said. "I'm usually the one drinking a lot!"

"Yes, but maybe you're getting older and realising that being responsible is a nice trait to have," said Evelin.

They gave each other a high five and started to sing. Olivia looked at Andrew and winked.

"These two are switching characters," said Andrew. "I'm not sure if this is a good idea!"

"Oh, it's fine," Olivia reassured him with a huge smile. "It's fine if it's only for tonight."

They finally arrived at the venue, a grand building lit-up with neon lights decorating the canopy, covering its entrance, which had a red carpet.

"Look – a red carpet entry," she squealed with excitement. "We're on a red zone tonight…so let's have some fun!"

They entered the venue, where Olivia bumped into Mark and Stephanie. She wondered whether they were a couple, given that they were always together. Wishing them a good evening, she vowed to ensure her friends behaved themselves as she couldn't afford for there to be any gossip at work the following week.

The night went swimmingly until Evelin threw a glass of champagne over a man's face. He wasn't happy and started to shout and scream, which is when Olivia asked Andrew to help and find out what had happened. The man was escorted out of the building and Evelin, her face as red as the carpet, she had trodden on just a few hours earlier, told Andrew how the incident unfolded.

Evelin was shocked at how rude the man was. Having approached her and asked her for a dance, she refused and said thank you...but the man wasn't ready to take no for an answer. A nice, calm English rose, Evelin didn't like arrogant people. She wasn't in the least bit aggressive, so the man must have pushed a wrong button to make her snap like that. Olivia gave her a hug and suggested they continue the party at her house. Even Anna, who wasn't normally easily fazed, panicked. She had always said that alcohol was a provoked adrenaline that couldn't be controlled and tonight she agreed with Olivia's suggestion to party elsewhere.

They all left together with Andrew taking a separate cab home. In Anna's car, Evelin fell asleep on the way home.

"This is all probably a little too much for her," said Anna, looking at Olivia. "Maybe it's best to go home rather than continuing at your house."

"Yes, you're right – let's drop Evelin home first," said Olivia.

Anna nodded. "Poor Andrew – what a little drama for him tonight."

"Yes. And what a little drama for all of us," Olivia continued. "Hannah didn't join us tonight – do you think they're both okay?"

"I feel that something is happening between them, though I don't know what. But, Olivia, stop worrying about everybody. If there was something wrong, believe me when I say you'd be the first to know – you're his best friend."

"Yes, you're right – I'm too analytical," she said, bringing the matter to a close.

In the aftermath of her night out, Olivia gave all of her attention to the collection. The pressure was getting more intense as the show grew closer. Her first fashion show for the company was just a few weeks away and would be staged in London. Her team was very excited and had all worked hard – so much so that, at this stage, only final preparations of the samples were left to do.

Olivia had, somehow, managed to keep everything on schedule. The combination of pressure and anticipation really worked for her and she was addicted to it. She always loved such exciting yet stressful times, which were an adrenaline drag to her… though, as she received a call, she realised there were even more obstacles to surmount.

Olivia walked into the atelier and raising her voice a touch, asked her team to come closer. "I'm afraid I have some bad news. Our hand embroidery designer, Samantha, ended up in emergency today. She was riding her bicycle to work and had an accident. She's well, so don't panic but has fractured her right arm. We can arrange to visit her once we know where she'll be transferred if hospitalised. In our industry, we always have obstacles and unpredictable situations. Until today, everything has been running smoothly but we were bound to experience some problems. Now I have to place somebody else in charge and ensure that we remain on course with our schedule.'

Baptiste stepped forward and said in a convincing voice, "I know that I'm not an embroidery designer but I've done lots of embroidery in the company and have been in charge of it before. I'm happy to take responsibility and will continue to do my best to stay on schedule."

Olivia was surprised and pleased at the same time. Yes, she had her doubts about Baptiste but if he was willing to try and change her opinion of him, then good for him. She looked at her team and confirmed that she was happy for Baptiste to be in charge of the embroidered samples from now on. Everybody agreed and cheered for Baptiste and Olivia thought, *If he can deliver the task on time with no sarcasm or a grumpy attitude, then everybody's a winner.*

Olivia returned to her office and her team got on with their work. She opened the board containing all of the embroidered designs to try and devise contingency plans, should there be any more emergencies without taking anything out. While she focused on the board, she heard a knock on the door.

"Come in," she said to find Baptiste entering her office.

"I just wanted a quick chat with you," he began. "About earlier. Maybe you don't totally agree with me taking charge of the situation but as I've said, I have great knowledge and experience in embroidery. I did two other collections before, where my main focus was on the embroidery aspect of the designs. Besides, I think I can be of more help than I've been so far this season."

"Baptiste, I'm fine with you taking on more responsibility," Olivia responded. "And if you feel that you can help more, well, that's even better for the team. I have no issues with you and hope you don't have any either. I've given a little freedom to the team and apportioned specific tasks to everybody because the only way to see how well a person performs is when somebody gives them a chance.

"I'm aware that you prefer to have bigger responsibilities and like to be in charge but at the same time, you know that over the years working in the company, if nobody had given you a chance to show how good you are, then you would've left a long time ago. It's the same with everybody. We all deserve chances and encouragement. We all want to grow and succeed."

Baptiste stepped a little closer and, for first time, since she began working for the firm, Olivia saw a little smile on his face – maybe he had realised what a fun colleague she was with good leadership skills.

"Do you mind if I show you what we can do, in case we have any difficulties with some of the embroidered designs?"

It was the first time Baptiste had spoken to Olivia in a normal voice with no sarcasm or anger. They sat down and went over the embroidered designs for several hours. With such little time left, it was very important that situations like this were handled calmly. They finalised some little changes and Baptiste gave Olivia a high five with a huge smile on his face.

Olivia ordered a quick lunch over the phone, then went to the conference room, where in an hour's time, she would be having a very important meeting in relation to the show. Every fashion brand, high end or couture, had a themed setting organised for a show. In this case, Olivia had been preparing for several months and it was fast approaching the point where all of her planning would come to life.

With the technology so advanced, she already had the setting of the show on 3D, created by a great in-house team. It looked out of the ordinary – something special that hadn't been done before. She always loved the idea of creating a setting for a fashion show like Karl Lagerfeld did for Chanel and Fendi and with everything ready for the meeting, a satisfied Olivia went to the kitchen to grab the lunch she had ordered.

Olivia had invited Sarah and her team, key marketing people, PR and other departments relevant to the setting of the show. She wanted to get their reaction to it, having always believed that while one mind could be fabulous, magic could result when everybody brought their thoughts to the table.

After eating her lunch, Olivia rushed to the conference room, where everyone was gathered. Greeting them with a broad smile, she began her address, "Hello, everyone, and thank you for coming along. I bet you're curious as to what happens next and this is a great opportunity for us to look at the setting, study the details and, if necessary, brainstorm to make it even better. So, let's look at the 3D version of the setting and let it speak for itself."

Everybody in the room was totally fascinated by the 3D setting and Sarah reinforced Olivia's confidence in it with words that further inspired her. "That's why you're our creative director. Only an extraordinary mind can come up with such a setting. I'm very much looking forward to seeing the show and cherishing the moment. This season will be very special for our company and I'd like to thank you all."

Olivia had great feedback from everyone. She hadn't expected the reaction to be so positive and left the room feeling energised. With another appointment to run to before the day ended, she invited Baptiste to join her at the atelier. A few samples had to be finalised that day and Olivia wanted to ensure that everything was under control.

Baptiste was waiting for her downstairs at reception, having offered to drive her to the atelier. Olivia felt that they finally had a chance to work together on the samples and to bond properly as a team and with little traffic on the road, the journey didn't take very long at all. Simultaneously entering the atelier, Sid and Silvia looked surprised to see them together. Pretty much everybody in the company had heard that they didn't get on but Olivia hoped that they would find something else to gossip about by inviting Baptiste to join her.

They sat down, analysing every sample from the fitting to the very last little detail. It was nice to see Baptiste in his element, making jokes and commenting on the garments.

Time flew by and Olivia stood up and said, "I'm so happy with the progress we've made so far. Despite the embroidery having minor issues, it's great to see how far we've come. Great team work, so well done to you all."

Sid and Silvia confirmed that they were confident of the samples being ready on time and, with that in mind, Olivia and Baptiste left the atelier. On the way to the car, Baptiste thanked Olivia for inviting him to join her. He seemed to have genuinely warmed to her, seeing her as a colleague and a friend and by the time they arrived back at the office, it was after 8 pm. Baptiste left straight away, making for home after telling Olivia he had a little issue with his partner and that it was better to resolve it as soon as possible.

Olivia left the office too. With a 6 am start, it had been a long day and she looked forward to a nice bath and a good sleep.

My goodness, doesn't time fly – I can't believe the show is taking place tomorrow, Olivia thought to herself. The adrenaline rushing through her had been so intense that she hadn't had time to count the days. She looked at her phone and decided to call Andrew. "I'm just calling to double check if you're all coming together to the show?" she asked once he answered.

"Yes, we are," replied Andrew. "How are you getting on with the last-minute preparations?"

"Everything's under control," she said, trying to contain her enthusiasm. "There's lots of pressure but I'm very excited. It'll be a great, unique show and something the company hasn't done before. I hope it'll satisfy the clients and the press."

"We'll be there to support you. Knowing your creative talent and desire for perfection, I don't doubt it will be one of the most beautiful collections I've ever seen. Let us know if there's anything we can do from our side to help."

"Thank you to you all for being there for me," said Olivia. "This is the biggest source of help and support that I have."

"Great, see you tomorrow," said Andrew.

Olivia ended the call and feeling the need for a short meditation, sat down for a few minutes and closed her eyes. Lost in a world of calm, it was only when hearing a knock on her door that she opened them again. "Come in."

Michael opened the door and entered, looking nervous.

"Is everything okay?" asked Olivia.

"Yes…well, apart from one thing. You have two meetings at the same time and it's my fault – I should have double checked. In an hour, it'll be the last rehearsal for the catwalk and half-an-hour later, the CEO of the company is arriving from the airport for tomorrow's show."

"Never mind," said Olivia. "Maybe it's meant to be – he can see the end of the rehearsals and, you never know, he might want to have a little input before the show. Don't worry, at this stage these are minor things. Just make sure that other stuff like last minute repairs or completion of the samples is finished tonight, not tomorrow morning. Oh and check on the models – maybe you can cheer them up with a little surprise after rehearsals. We need to guarantee that everybody is happy for the big day."

"Of course," said Michael. "What about you – do you need anything else?"

"I'll let you know if I need anything else from you," said Olivia. "You already have lots to do."

"Okay," smiled Michael. "I'll get on with my work."

With Michael having left her office, Olivia went to the powder room to refresh herself before leaving for the venue where the show was taking place. She wanted to get there a little early before everybody else arrived for the rehearsals. She looked at herself in the mirror and noticed the deep, dark circles under her eyes. Then smiled and thought, *You, little workaholic devil, you have to start looking after yourself – you aren't in your 20s anymore! You need to have a mask before bed and will look a trillion dollars tomorrow, baby.*

As planned, Olivia arrived early and went to talk to the team that was still building the set for the following day.

"How are you getting on?" she asked Victor, a muscular man in his 40s, who had tattoos on his forearms.

"We're almost there." He smiled. "There's still a few bits and bobs to do but I promise everything will be ready by tonight."

"I'll keep that in mind," said Olivia. "We need to ensure that nothing is left for tomorrow. Send me an email once you're finished, in case I'm not around."

She turned and walked to the middle of the catwalk stage, envisaging a packed audience. The room and runaway looked so beautiful already, even without the final additions. Leaving the stage, she sat in one of the seats laid out, visualising the show as it unfolded.

As she did, Baptiste showed up, greeting her in his native tongue: "Bonjour, Madame Olivia!"

"Bonjour, Monsieur Baptiste," said Olivia with a smile. "The runaway is almost finished."

"And doesn't it look great? I can really picture the show now."

"Yes, me too," said Olivia. "I can't believe it's almost over…then we move on to another adventure for next season."

"Fashion never takes a break!" Grinned Baptiste.

"Yes, but we're all on a lifelong holiday here as there's nothing better than loving what you do on a daily basis."

"Agreed! Right, I'll go and check on the models – I love chatting to them."

"I know…and they love talking to you too!" Smiled Olivia.

How fabulous is that? Thought Olivia. *It's the night before the show and everything is on course with no drama or unexpected shocks.* She glanced around to see the venue getting busier as people arrived for the rehearsals.

"Ah, here you are," said Sid, stepping towards her. "I've been looking for you. The models are getting ready – is that okay?"

"No, I want to see them on the stage before they get ready," said Olivia. "It's better if we finish the catwalk and the rest of the show before the final rehearsal. I'll come with you backstage. I thought I made that clear to Michael and everybody else involved."

They both rushed back stage, where almost all of her team were gathered, including Samantha.

"Hi, Samantha, what a surprise," said Olivia.

"I couldn't miss the rehearsals," Samantha replied. "We've worked so hard to get here. I might not be able to help but I can at least support you all."

"You look great. Well done for coming down. How is your hand, by the way?"

"It's much better, thank you. You've all spoiled me with the visits, flowers and cards. I very much appreciate that."

"You've been missed," said Olivia. "Baptiste has done a great job with the embroidery, following all of your work and advice." She spoke a little more loudly than usual, so that everybody could hear her. "As planned, let's all go to the main room, apart from the beautiful models. We can all pretend to be the audience and watch the girls walking on the runway. I need your opinions, so don't be shy. And if any of you have any suggestions or ideas, they are welcome."

They all sat down and the room went dark. Beautiful house music started to play in the background and, one by one, the models walked the runway. Olivia and her colleagues sat in silence, observing. Olivia thought it magical to be in the shoes of the audience…but it was now time for the models to wear the samples. She decided to stay in the room rather than going backstage to help the models prepare, as this was her only chance to see the rehearsed show.

When the models were ready to begin strutting down the catwalk, Michel announced that the company's CEO had arrived on the premises. Olivia raised her voice, asking for a five-minute break before the rehearsal started, wanting to make sure that Sarah and the CEO were in the room. Rushing backstage to see if everybody was ready, she hurried back to join her colleagues in the audience.

Spotting Sarah standing next to a tall, broad-shouldered man wearing an immaculately tailored suit and freshly polished shoes, Olivia approached them.

"Hi, and welcome to the rehearsals," she said by way of a greeting.

"Thank you," said the suited man, who offered her his hand. "You must be Olivia. My name's Simon and I'm the company's CEO."

"Very pleased to meet you." Smiled Olivia, slipping her much smaller hand into his palm to shake. "And how are you, Sarah?"

"Very well, thank you," she said. "How are things going here?"

"Good – I hope! We're about to find out," Olivia replied, glancing at Michael, who made a sign that everybody was ready. "Please, take a seat."

In no time, the lights went off and the music started to play. As the first models stepped onto the catwalk, the room gradually became bathed in a beautiful lilac colour. The designs looked so striking on the statuesque figures of the models with the collection's Roman theme working beautifully on the runway. It was so magical and surreal, the models looking like goddesses and Amazons. The music synced wonderfully with the lights, which reflected an entire day, moving from early morning to sunset. It was a great, dramatic, powerful theme and Olivia felt so proud of herself and her team for solving the puzzle that the collection had represented.

Walking onstage, she started to speak, "Now, that was magical! I'm so proud of everybody who helped and worked with me to deliver this special moment. I know that tomorrow we can deliver a great show."

Simon stood up and started clapping and everybody else followed.

"That was simply dreamlike – extraordinary!" Gushed Sarah.

"This is only the beginning," Simon declared. "I'm proud and happy with such results. Our big family is the most talented out there – well done, Olivia and the entire team. What you've delivered here today is very powerful. But I can't expect any less than that from now on!" He concluded with a smile after which everybody cheered and laughed.

Olivia wanted to bring Baptiste and the rest of her team onstage to celebrate the success of the rehearsals but thought better of it. Yes, it was a fantastic start but tomorrow was their acid test and she would save her most flattering remarks if the show itself went as well – or, she hoped, even better. "Has anyone got any comments or suggestions on how we might improve the show for tomorrow?"

Simon gave her a thumbs-up. "I think you're capable of excellence, Olivia. We think the show is just perfect."

"Thank you," cried Olivia, who cuddled the models. "For all of us, the show has taken place today...but for the whole world, it'll be tomorrow!"

Chapter Four
A Tested Emotional Bond Is a Friendship That Lasts Forever

For the first time in a little while, Olivia woke up and felt lonely – sad, even, for no apparent reason – as she looked through the window. She occasionally had this feeling but was at a loss to explain it; though she had the distinct impression that it would pass…and that once she had the chance to clear her mind, something good was going to happen, which would change her life in some way. She had always felt that she had a sixth sense, which every so often resurfaced to guide her.

More reflective than would normally be the case, with it being a Sunday, Olivia was ready to meditate…to try and really relax. She reminded herself that there was no reason for her to feel even remotely sad, her hard work having paid off to see her first collection greatly received. Now it was time for her to balance her life a little and set herself up for a fabulous week ahead.

It had taken years of practice for her to reach the stratum of meditation she was now able to slip rather effortlessly into. In that plane of consciousness, she was able to control and shift her emotions which, when moulded in the right way, felt more like superpowers. Her guilty pleasure, it was a place where she felt safe. While in the physical world, she had her creativity, her friends, the love of reading about philosophy, psychology and science but in that special place, she could be whoever or whatever she wanted.

She remained marooned there until the chime of her doorbell rang out, catapulting her back into reality. *Who's looking for me on a Sunday morning?* She thought. Answering the door, a beaming Anna stood with a Starbucks coffee in one hand and breakfast in the other.

"Surprise," she said with a huge smile on her face. "I know you like to sleep in on Sundays but thought this would be great for a change!"

"What a nice surprise," said Olivia. "Come on in! Actually, I was meditating when you rang the bell. Oh, well, no meditation for me today."

"How about some healthy gossip instead? I think it's a better form of dopamine – for me, at least."

"You know I don't like gossiping but if you say it's a healthy one, it must be very interesting!"

They looked at each other and laughed, heading into the lounge.

"You'll like this one – at least, I think you will," said Anna.

"Okay, let's hear it then," said Olivia, who sat down in her favourite chair. "Now I'm getting curious. Is this a joke or do you actually have something to say?"

"Yes, I have," Anna continued. "But you must prepare yourself because it's a little sad…although I'm not."

"Did something happen?" asked Olivia.

"Andrew broke up with Hannah – for good, from what I understand. She's already moved out and they are amicable about it."

"This is shocking," said a surprised Olivia. "I don't know what to say. Why didn't he tell me? I thought we were best friends."

"He didn't want to distract you or ruin the fashion show. You know how he cares about you. I'm sure he'll talk to you this week. I just wanted to let you know before you see him. At least now you can decide how best to support him and his decision."

"You say he ended the relationship but this doesn't make sense. I thought the next step for them was marriage. I'm flabbergasted. You're absolutely right – this is sad and I need to talk to him now."

"Please, take it easy. I know he's having breakfast with Hannah today, so maybe call him in a few hours. He's really trying to remain friends with her. From what I understand, they lost the spark for each other and I think Hannah is already dating somebody else."

"How come you know so much about it and I don't know anything?" Olivia wanted to know. "Is it because he kept it secret from everybody until the night of the show?"

"He was a little tipsy, which is rare and he opened up about his situation. He wanted to tell you first but the drink must've made him blurt it out. Don't get upset – things like that happen."

"I understand. It's just that I didn't sense anything going on, apart from last time, when we went out before the show. Hannah was supposed to join us but didn't show up, which made me think something was wrong. But because he reassured me that everything was fine, I forgot about it."

"I don't mean any disrespect towards Hannah because I like her – she's a great girl. But I have butterflies for you both because I think you and Andrew are meant to be together – your bond is so pure and powerful."

"Yes, it is – but a friendship bond. Many years ago, I had different feelings but they all vanished. He needs my support right now. I'm his best friend and I didn't realise anything was wrong. My life became so hectic and selfish that I focused too much on myself rather than being around the people I love," said Olivia, giving Anna a huge hug.

"Don't punish yourself – it's not your fault. You need to focus on your life and career. We all do and sometimes we get caught up in stuff. Sometimes life is like that, and you, more than any of us, know that."

"I'm impressed with your speech, my dear philosopher friend," said Olivia.

"Well, I did tell you that healthy gossip is in fashion right now," joked Anna.

They smiled and set about eating their breakfast.

"Does Evelin know anything about it?" asked Olivia.

"No, she doesn't. We didn't want to tell her – you know how emotional she gets. At least if we all know, it'll be easier to handle her."

"You're right, she's such a sensitive soul sometimes. How's your work and life in general?"

"Everything's fine. Nothing new or exciting at the moment. I'm traveling abroad next week for a few days for work. That should be fine – new faces, new environment…I like that." Grinned Anna.

After breakfast, Olivia kept looking at her phone. The only thing in her mind was Andrew and what she should do to help and support him. The hours flew by at such a rate that it was about 1 pm when Anna's phone rang.

Before speaking to him, she whispered the caller's identity – "It's Andrew!" – which prompted Olivia into pacing from one side of the room to the other. After a couple of minutes of listening, Anna started to speak, "Andrew, I'm at Olivia's and she knows everything."

"What are you doing there?" He barked angrily – so loudly, in fact, that Olivia could hear his voice, which made her feel even more ill at ease. "And why have you told her?"

"Don't talk to me like that!" Anna raged. "I did you a favour – you didn't tell her and she would've found out sooner or later anyway. Look, she's standing next to me if you want a word?"

Olivia grabbed the phone from Anna and strode towards the window. Inhaling deeply, she peered out of it and readied herself to speak. "Hi, Andrew."

"Hi, Olivia. I'm sorry I didn't tell you about me and Hannah but I've had a lot to process and haven't really been myself."

"I'm not mad at you," said Olivia. "And I understand why you didn't want to tell me. Calm down, everything will be fine. We're here to support you – why don't you come over and join us for a coffee?"

"Sure, that's good of you," said Andrew in a calmer voice. "I'll start making my way over. See you in a bit."

Olivia put the phone down and looked at Anna. "You probably figured out that he's coming over now."

"That's great. I'm sorry I told you – that he wanted to talk to you first – but I thought that by spilling the beans, we could figure out how to support him together. You're so kind and caring."

"I must admit that I'm grateful you told me before Andrew. I would've panicked and maybe argued with him, instead of supporting him. You know me so well."

"Yes, I do." Smiled Anna. "And, believe me, it took me hours to think about and decide what to do. I knew Andrew would get mad at me but this way we can all sit and talk together."

Olivia nodded. "Well, I don't know how many hours you've been thinking because you only found out last night. It's great that it happened this way. I know you very well too – you can't keep secrets for long. Your great mind can't digest this kind of thing on its own. You need company, my dear, darling Anna."

"Yes, you're right – I can't argue with that! Do you have a bottle of wine? I think maybe that'll be handy."

"Yes, of course. In fact, I have Andrew's favourite. But isn't it a bit early for alcohol?" She thought for a moment. "Unless we decide to have lunch in?"

"Let's play it by ear and see how it goes," said Anna.

The doorbell rang, Olivia walking into the hall to answer. Opening the door, she met with the sight of Andrew, who held a tray of take-out coffees and a big note saying, "I'm sorry."

"Come in, Andrew," said Olivia. "Don't hide."

As Andrew walked in, placing the coffees on a table in the hall, Anna approached and gave him a huge hug. "This is my 'I'm sorry' hug," she said.

"That'll do, you terrible secret keeper," said Andrew, walking towards Olivia. He hugged her and kissed her on her cheek.

"Are you okay?" she asked. "How was your breakfast with Hannah?"

"It went well. I don't know how much Anna has told you about it but we're totally fine. I think because she's dating this guy from her work place, it somehow helped to ease the situation and make it more amicable for us both. When I first found out, I was angry but the more I thought about it, the more it made sense." Andrew sat down and continued, "You probably sensed something was up…that we've been dragging our relationship out for too long. Hannah's a great girl and a wonderful person but unfortunately we grew apart. She was more focused on her job and friends and, to be fair, it was something I was guilty of too."

"I understand all of this but you can't just split like this. Maybe you just need a break from each other?"

"I hear you, Olivia, but this time it's over for real. We still love and respect each other and, I hope, will remain great friends."

"We're here for you, Andrew, and we respect your decision," said Anna. "If you need a shoulder to cry on, I'm a great one but Olivia is probably the best – she's your best friend, after all."

"Thank you for not giving me huge headaches." Sighed Andrew. "I was a little afraid of talking to you all. Now I realise I shouldn't have, been as great friends always stick together and are there for each other, no matter what."

Anna and Olivia echoed the final part of his last sentence, drawing a smile from Andrew.

"I'm glad that none of us have forgotten our golden rule," said Olivia.

After a little while, Anna left to attend a meeting. Olivia and Andrew had lunch together and sat down for hours. Olivia patiently listened to Andrew, who clearly needed to offload some emotional energy in further discussing everything that had been happening recently. She wanted to interrupt him many times to disagree but chose instead to remain calm and silent, knowing that, while everybody had their opinion, it was sometimes more important to just listen and be there for whoever needed her most.

By the time it was late afternoon – when Olivia usually took Duke for a long walk – she asked if Andrew would like to join them.

"After so many hours listening to my crazy stories, you still want me to join you and Duke for a walk?"

"Of course!"

"I'd love to but I have lots of work to do as I have a presentation tomorrow."

"I understand," said Olivia. "No matter what happens, life continues and we have to do our best. Let's talk more often from now on, please. This conversation has reminded me how important our friendship is. After all these years, our friendship never disappointed or failed. I love that and will cherish it forever."

Andrew embraced Olivia. "Thank you for being there for me when I need you the most. I'll talk to you tomorrow at some point."

"Great. And don't forget to let me know how your presentation goes. If you need any guidance from the design perspective, let me know – I'm always happy to help."

"Yes, boss!" Grinned Andrew, who gave Olivia a kiss before leaving.

Olivia closed the door and for a minute sat by the door, thinking deeply. When Duke bounced towards her, tail wagging, she couldn't help but laugh.

"Who wants to go for a walk? I think maybe Duke and his naughty mama, who has neglected him today."

Duke's tail wagged furiously as he ran around Olivia. She grabbed his harness and gave him a treat, which he wolfed down.

"This is for you, for being such a good boy today," she said.

Going out with Duke was always a joy – fresh air and walking in silence with her loving pet was greatly therapeutic. *Andrew and Hannah must be caught up in emotion right now*, she thought. *Despite everything looking fine on the surface, they had been struggling and separating from a partner after so many years must be painful and confusing. I must talk to Hannah.*

She turned a corner to walk Duke onto a massive field, where the locals brought their dogs. Today, however, it was very quiet with most people visiting in the morning or evening.

Olivia looked at Duke and said, "I'm sorry, buddy. It seems as if you don't have any friends out today. I'll try and compensate by playing with you – how about running together?"

Playing with Duke was such a special feeling that Olivia forgot all about what had happened with Andrew and Hannah. Duke hugged and loved her no matter what and, after giving him a cuddle, they enjoyed a good hour of running and jumping. Tired out, they were both happy to go back home.

Sunday was almost over and Olivia decided to prepare dinner for herself and Duke. At weekends, she prepared special treats for him – *he was her baby forever*, she thought, looking at him, then gave him a kiss on his long, soft ears.

The next day, Olivia woke early in readiness for work – due to such an unexpected weekend, she hadn't managed to prepare her schedule for the week ahead. Walking out of the house, it was a sunny but chilly morning with autumn having already arrived. Reaching her office quicker than she anticipated, she grabbed a coffee from the kitchen and rushed to get her weekly plan done. For the first time since starting work with The Delaney Brothers, she found her office quiet and cosy. Olivia loved being surrounded by people but today it was perfect like that.

The day zoomed by at such a speed that it seemed over before it had even begun. Several people had taken time off after weeks of nonstop commitment, which made the building a lot quieter. In many ways, it helped Olivia focus, preparing her schedule a month in advance and starting to look over the predicted colours and trends.

Fashion moved so quickly that nothing felt personal anymore with so many designs replicated and very little originality. The fashion world used to feel like one big family and Olivia's dream had been to become a great designer like Dior or Valentino. But gaining such success felt almost impossible – the industry had changed so much, becoming more corporate in nature and much larger…to the extent that you could only really make it if you became part of one of the few companies which controlled the luxury and couture world.

Before leaving the office for the day, Olivia called Andrew to see how he was.

"I'm fine, but busy," he answered a little abruptly. "I'll call you tomorrow at some point."

Olivia sensed some hostility on his part but told herself she had caught him at a bad moment and would check on him the following day. Once home, she made a fuss of Duke and made herself a mint tea when her doorbell rang. Answering, she found Andrew on her doorstep, looking angry and sad. "Hello, Andrew," she said, opening the door for him to enter the house. "Can I get you a tea or a glass of wine?"

"Can I have a glass of wine, please?" asked a frowning Andrew, who looked troubled, sitting in the living room.

"Is everything okay with you?" asked Olivia, handing him a glass of wine. "You sounded stressed when we spoke earlier."

"I don't know anymore," he said. "Yesterday, I seemed to have worked things through in my head, especially after talking to you but it seems as if everything is collapsing. Hannah had an argument with her new man and claims that was because of me – I'm being blamed for being calm and relaxed about this, would you believe?" He sighed and looked directly at Olivia. "Sorry for being short on the phone – I was having a drink with her after work. I'm trying so hard to make this situation as amicable as possible but think it's getting out of hand. Maybe I should stop contacting her now and get on with my life." Andrew necked his glass of wine. "Can I have another?"

Olivia sat next to him. "Try to calm down. We women are confusing sometimes. We can't control our emotions and have to let it all out. I don't believe she meant what she said. It takes time to get over a feeling that you had for a long time and as always, it's easy to blame the other person. Sometimes we upset people with the wrong words but we don't really mean them."

"Yes, you're right. How come you know so much about it? You only had a reasonably long-term relationship with Adam."

"Well," Olivia began, remembering her first love. "I learned a lot in a relatively short space of time and I'm very intuitive. And, because I'm a sensitive, analytical person, I can't do it again. It's too emotional and it drains you. But it's hard to compare my relationship of three years with yours of over 11. Hannah has been your partner for a long time. Okay, so maybe you've grown apart but you still have your memories…you know each other's habits and how to comfort one another. I bet in the evenings when you're alone, you think of it and ask yourself if the decision you made was right."

"I definitely know that I made the right decision. It's just hard in general," said Andrew, raising his glass. "Do you have another bottle of this delicious wine?"

"No, but I have a great bottle of Port. How about I open that to have with some cheese?"

"That's a great idea," said Andrew.

Olivia poured what was left of the wine into Andrew's glass, then went into the kitchen to open the Port. As she uncorked the Port, she felt a presence behind her, turning to see Andrew standing there. Stepping forward, he gave her a huge hug.

"Thank you for helping and supporting me." He smiled. "You're an angel."

"You know how much I value my friends," said Olivia, handing Andrew the Port. "Here, take this into the living room."

She sat in the kitchen for a few moments, feeling a little overwhelmed by the situation. Somehow, Andrew's hug felt different. They were best friends, yet the intensity of his embrace suggested he might want more. Trying to put her uncertainty to one side, she removed some cheese from the fridge and took it into the living room. She tried to look as calm as possible and sat down on the other side of the sofa to Andrew.

"Look, this is none of my business but I think all of this happened too quickly. That's why problems are only starting to occur now. Hannah probably started dating, purely to show you that she's fine and that she's moved on. Whether that's the truth, she probably doesn't know herself. It's a defensive reaction that we women have sometimes. Do you want me to talk to her? I'm happy to call her and maybe see her for a coffee before work?"

"I'm not convinced that's a good idea." Frowned Andrew. "But if you think it'll help, I don't mind. Despite our problems, she's a good woman and I want her to be happy."

"Okay, don't overthink this," said Olivia. "I'll arrange to see her tomorrow. Now, let's talk about something else – how was your day at work?"

"Hectic, but manageable," Andrew replied. "Lots of changes are happening in the company. A big American firm has acquired a huge share in it, so it'll probably be a year or so before everything settles down."

"Wow, you're having double trouble in your life right now. I hope things will get easier in time. The most important thing is for you to be truthful to yourself."

"I'm actually glad that all of this is happening at once. Being busy helps keep my mind on other things. And what about you – how's work going?"

"Today was very quiet compared to normal, as we have a lot of staff holidays being taken at the same time. I've managed to arrange my monthly schedule and started to look at all of the predicted trends and pantone colours, trying to get an idea of what everybody will be focusing on."

"You and your regimented time," joked Andrew. "Is your discipline a gift or have you worked out a way to control it?"

"I don't know – both, I suppose!" Then, changing the subject, she asked, "What about Evelin? It's about time we saw her again."

"True. Maybe we should have dinner after work one evening – here, locally, as you know she's not really a city girl anymore."

"That's a great idea! Why don't you invite her and let us know what day and time?"

"Leave it to me," said Andrew. "I'll arrange it, though don't say anything to Anna, otherwise she's bound to let the cat out of the bag and do more damage! Not that she did with me, to be fair – she knows me so well. Her spilling the beans was probably for the best – you know how I react when I'm in shock."

"Instead of being supportive, I might have told you off for not trusting in me."

"Well, you telling me off sounds familiar! But, really, thank you for being there for me. I really enjoyed today – the wine, Port and…well, just talking. It really does help."

"You know I'm always here for you," said Olivia. "Let me know how it goes with Hannah."

"Sure – will do." He checked the time. "I must leave now. You're such a great friend," he added standing up.

"My pleasure. You're like a brother to me."

"Only that?" asked Andrew, looking straight into her eyes.

For a second or two, Olivia didn't know what to say.

"I'm only messing with you," smiled Andrew, who gave Olivia another hug before leaving.

Olivia sat down and thought, *Was Andrew really joking or was he testing me? I'm not sure about this as my sixth sense is a little fragile at the moment. Maybe that's a good thing and I shouldn't take it seriously.* She remembered her mint tea and went into the kitchen to finally prepare it, knowing it would help to calm her down and set her up for a nice, refreshing sleep.

And, indeed, it did exactly that, Olivia waking feeling reinvigorated. Calling Hannah a few minutes after rising, Olivia received no answer, so left a voicemail message asking if she fancied meeting for a coffee.

By the time she reached her office, Hannah sent her a text, explaining that she had been stuck in traffic when she called but that she would be glad to catch-up over a coffee. Olivia texted her back, asking if she could hook-up as soon as an hour's time and, if not, maybe tomorrow instead? "An hour is fine – how about the Ivy in Covent Garden?" came Hannah's response, to which Olivia responded,

"Perfect, see you there!"

Settling into her chair, Olivia buzzed Michael's extension. "Hi, Michael. Can you please come to my office to discuss my timetable?"

"Sure, see you in a bit."

A couple of minutes later, he entered her office, taking a seat.

"I have some stuff left to do today before noon. I know a few people are still off but if you can arrange a date with everybody, we need to have a meeting before we start our new schedule. I have a board meeting next week and I want to make sure that we're all on the same page with everything."

"That's fine, I'll get the staff done by noon and confirm the meeting by the end of the day. Let me know if you need any further assistance."

"I'm out for two/three hours but if anything important occurs, just call me."

"No problem. It's very quiet today on our floor, so a good time to do lots of work. I can't believe you didn't take yesterday off like so many others."

"You know me by now – I like my routine." Smiled Olivia.

Olivia was sitting in a black cab on her way to meeting Hannah, when her phone beeped. Andrew had sent a text message, saying that he had organised dinner with Evelin for Saturday that week. Olivia answered immediately, saying she was fine with that and while she wanted to let him know that she was on her way to meet Hannah, she thought better of it, considering it might be best for him not to know.

As she climbed out of the cab, Olivia was about to head for the Ivy when the driver beeped her.

"Is this your umbrella?" he asked.

"Typical!" Laughed Olivia. "This happens all the time!"

Olivia entered the restaurant to find Hannah sitting in the far-right corner, checking her phone. "Good morning!" she said by way of greeting, walking up to her.

Hannah stood up smiling and gave her a hug. "I've ordered a cappuccino with soya," she said. "I know you like your coffee and hope this is still your order."

"Yes, it is," said Olivia as she sat down. "Thank you."

"How's your work?" Hannah asked her. "I'm sorry I didn't manage to come and see your show but I heard it went amazingly well and that you're the main girl in the company."

"Thanks, Hannah. I'm not that high up – yet! But I am very much enjoying every moment of it. Fashion and creativity are in my blood."

Hannah looked at her and with sadness in her voice, said, "I assume you know that me and Andrew have moved on from our relationship. It sounds sad but I think it's for the best. We'd been great for each other for a long time but in the end I couldn't see a future for us. I know what great friends you are, so you probably know more than I think."

"Actually, I only found out a few days ago," said Olivia. "Andrew avoided saying anything until he was sure you were both happy to tell the world."

Hannah looked impressed. "That's nice to know. We're trying our best to handle the situation but it's not been easy. I care about him and, even now, fear losing him. I know it's selfish but I can't help it."

"Everything will be fine. Don't blame yourself, just give it a time and you'll see how your friendship will get better and stronger."

"That's easy for you to say because you're friends," said Hannah. "I don't even know if my dating right now is just a fling for attention or a real feeling. Maybe I've completely ruined our relationship."

"I doubt it," said Olivia. "It takes two sides for a relationship to work. If you started to see somebody else, it's because you didn't feel happy or fulfilled in your relationship with Andrew. We women don't do stuff like that unless we're pushed towards it. We're keepers and naturally nurturing human beings. And, Hannah, it's pointless torturing yourself. It won't make anything better – to the contrary, it'll have the opposite effect. We have to learn how to move on by keeping ourselves busy."

"Is that how you've handled the situation with Andrew?" asked Hannah raising her eyebrows. "Do you think I don't know that he always had a hidden love for you? For years, I thought it was me being jealous and whenever I confronted him about it, he always denied it and said it was only a friendship."

Olivia suddenly felt very hot under the collar. Standing, she looked Hannah in the eye. "I'm so sorry that you feel this way. I thought we were good friends and I've never tried to ruin your relationship. It's so sad that you feel like this – clearly, we think differently. I'm sorry you're going through such a painful time but it's not me you should be blaming or hating on. I came here to see how I can help both of you but I was clearly mistaken."

Close to tears, Olivia walked off the premises. She felt heartbroken and elected against catching a cab back to work. Instead, she walked the streets of London, wondering what she had done to make Hannah feel so hostile towards her. She heard a car beeping but didn't register that it was for her until it pulled up right next to her and a rather handsome man in a nice grey suit, who looked to be in his mid-60s, stared at her.

"Do you want to commit suicide, young lady? I've been beeping you to cross over onto the pavement but you gave me no reaction at all."

"I'm so sorry," said Olivia. "I didn't realise it was for me – I was in my own world. My deepest apologies."

"That's fine – not a problem at all. You're walking on a very dangerous road. I can give you a lift or help stop a cab for you."

"Thank you, that's very kind of you," Olivia responded. "I'll grab a cab as soon as I have the chance."

"I can see one on the way," the gentleman said, stepping out of his beautiful Lamborghini sport supercar. "I'll stop it for you." Whistling and raising a hand, the taxi ground to a halt beside them. "Can you take this young lady wherever she needs to go?" he asked the driver, then turned to face Olivia. "My name is John Spencer."

"Nice to meet you, Mr Spencer," said Olivia, shaking his hand. "Thank you for saving me today!" She wanted to tell him that her second name was Spencer but then thought she had better jump in the cab to avoid creating a traffic jam.

"Not at all – you seemed miles away. Try and have a nice rest of the day," he said driving off.

Olivia didn't get the chance to respond, the Lamborghini racing off. Climbing into the cab, Olivia sat in the back, embarrassed that her musing had almost caused an accident. London traffic was so dangerous and carelessly walking on a road wouldn't give her a long lifespan. Not wanting to worsen her mood, she realised she had, on more than one occasion, met people with the same name, which she took as a sign of what, she didn't know, but she didn't believe in coincidences.

Once the cab had dropped her back to her place of work, Olivia went straight to her office. She didn't fancy speaking to anybody and felt a little stunned by what had happened earlier. *I need a short meditation*, she thought and hoped Andrew didn't ask about her meeting Hannah – and that she didn't mention it either. *Never mind, Olivia, you have to be stronger and bigger than this*, she thought. *At the end of the day, deep inside you know who you are, so stop feeling sorry for yourself. There are more important things in life and being weak isn't one of them.*

With that in mind, Olivia sat down on her office sofa and relaxed. Closing her eyes, she drifted somewhere far, far away…and when she opened her eyes, she felt infused with positive energy. A knock on the door fully brought her back to reality and she asked whoever it was to enter. In walked Baptiste, who had in his hands two glasses and a bottle of champagne.

"Please, don't say anything. I know how focused and organised you are but today, right now, we'll relax a little and toast you for what you've done here since you joined us."

Olivia was surprised to see him so happy and decided to go with the flow. Baptiste poured them each a glass, then raised his.

"I have a little confession to make and a toast at the same time. When I first met you, I honestly hated you and the idea of you too…not that you were mean or bad, or that anything was wrong with you. It was all me – I was afraid of the idea of you taking over this great place. But the more I started to get to know you, the more I felt guilty about hating you and retaliating like a horrible, unprofessional brat. But you've managed to understand me and changed my dreadful behaviour. You're not only a great designer, you're a great friend, and an unbelievable, inspirational visionary to all of us here."

Olivia wanted to interrupt him but decided to let Baptiste continue, appreciating his honesty.

"I want you to know that I'll be there for you, no matter what you need me for. Cheers to the amazing future that awaits, to the great success we achieved together, and to the one that we'll keep making!"

Olivia raised her glass. "Cheers to us!"

They sat down on the sofa and talked and laughed for a good hour. Olivia never thought that she and Baptiste could become so amicable but their friendship had grown in the time that she had been there and nowadays they shared giggles regularly. And that day, of all days, she really needed to hear what Baptiste had told her. *See, what happens when you don't let negative energy take over,* she told herself.

Once work was finished for the day, Olivia made her way towards her car when her phone rang and Andrew's name and number appeared on its screen.

"Hi, how are you today?" she asked.

"I'm fine…a little better today, as no phone calls or funny messages."

"Glad to hear it. What are you organising for Saturday evening? Is Anna coming as well?"

"I don't know yet. I left her a voicemail message, though I'm sure she'll be happy to join us."

"That's great. What about Evelin?"

"I just asked her to join us for dinner and didn't say anything about Hannah and I. I think it's better this way and, anyway, I'm meeting her for drinks beforehand, so I can tell her myself then, before we have dinner."

"Sounds like a good plan," said Olivia. "I'm looking forward to seeing you all on Saturday."

"Same here. I'll talk to you tomorrow."

"Okay, have a nice evening," said Olivia, who was glad Hannah didn't feature in their conversation, Andrew's brief mention aside. It wasn't the right time to discuss their altercation and she didn't want to worry Andrew, who already had a lot on his plate. And, as she pulled up onto her driveway, she received a text from Evelin, asking if everything was okay that Andrew had invited her out for drinks and dinner after and that she was looking forward to seeing everybody on Saturday. Olivia smiled and thought, *What would life be without my dear friends? I love them all so much.*

The week went by very quickly and, in no time, it was Saturday morning. Olivia looked in her wardrobe, choosing a bright, colourful yoga outfit. Kissing Duke, she left in a hurry for her yoga class. She felt happy and the colour of her outfit reflected her mood. At the studio, she spotted Anna from far away, slowly crept up on her and, like a child, wanted to scare her…but Anna looked behind her and foiled her.

"Ha – got you! Unfortunately, you can't hide with this bright colour on. I love it, though – neon blue suits you."

"Ah, thank you. How was your week?"

"Rather hectic but nice. My trip abroad went well and I met a very interesting young man on the plane."

"You'll never change!" Laughed Olivia.

"Yes, I'm happy where I am with my life." Drawing breath, she asked, "How are you? And how is Mr Heartbroken?"

"He seems to be fine and I'm great too. You're coming to dinner tonight, aren't you?"

"Oh, yes, I wouldn't miss it for the world. I'm curious how Andrew will talk to Evelin about what's happened. I hope they get tipsy before we meet for dinner as that way it'll be less drama."

They both took their place in the yoga class, readying themselves for a nice stretch and deep meditation. And that's exactly how the session transpired with both of them feeling relaxed and reinvigorated once it had finished.

In the evening, Anna offered to pick Olivia up so that they could travel together to the dinner. Olivia decided to go for smart casual, wearing black leather leggings, a beautiful baby blue blouse and a black blazer.

Opening the passenger door to Anna's car, she saw that she was wearing a beautiful structured dress in tomato red. "Now, that's what I call a dress and colour!"

"You inspired me with the neon colours at the yoga class today," said Anna. "I thought I'd surprise you and wear one of your beautiful designs."

"You look so radiant and beautiful," Olivia complimented her.

They arrived at a stunning country hotel in Surrey called Cliveden House. Leaving the car on valet, they stepped into the reception area.

Olivia looked at her, watch and said, "Why don't we have a drink before dinner?"

"Yes, I'm ready for a glass of champagne," said Anna.

As they ordered their drinks, Evelin appeared from nowhere. "I saw these glamorous ladies and thought, *I'll approach them!* She said, hugging the pair, "Andrew's coming as well – he's outside on the phone."

"How did your drinks go?" Olivia asked.

"The drinks were fine and the news was even better."

"What do you mean?" Anna asked.

"We were all afraid to talk to you, knowing how you normally react with no filter!"

"Well, surprise – this time I'm not reacting at all," said Evelin. "In fact, it was me who noticed something was missing in their relationship a long time ago. I always asked myself when they would both realise that, but it wasn't my place to get involved or say something."

"What a surprise," said Anna. "We'll have a nice evening now – I can smell it."

"Your sense of smell had better be good." Laughed Evelin. "I don't go out very often these days and when I do, I want to have the best time."

"We'll make sure it'll be a great evening for all of us," announced Andrew, who approached the girls with a beaming smile. "Now that you're all here and the table is ready, waiting for us, is anybody hungry?"

"We all are!" said Olivia.

"Great! After you, lovely ladies."

They entered the restaurant, which had a beautiful decor and a rather cosy feeling. Their table was by a window, which looked out over an amazingly lush, seemingly endless garden.

"Such a nice spot," said Anna.

They all sat down and ordered their drinks.

"Seeing all of us together, like a few weeks ago at Olivia's fashion show, is just amazing," said Andrew. "Thank you for making the effort. I know we've been talking about me and my relationship with Hannah for far too long, so now I want to raise a glass to our great friendship. You've all equally helped and supported me emotionally. I believe we're over the big, emotional stage and are trying to work out how to move on. Hannah's in a better place at the moment and has apologised for her childish behaviour."

Well, I'm glad she's in a better place, thought Olivia. *Despite what she said to me, I want her to be happy*.

"In fact, I have a video with her saying something to you all," Andrew continued.

He opened her recording, which had Hannah addressing them all, "Hello, everybody. I'm sorry for not keeping in touch but I'll be very happy to see you all very soon. Thank you for supporting Andrew – I'm a little jealous of what great friends he has! I'm now going to take a couple of months off to go travelling but once I'm back, I'll be in touch for a nice catch-up. Okay, bye for now, everybody."

"That's very sweet of her," said Anna. "I never really warmed to her properly but I'm happy to see her if she wants when she's back."

Their starters arrived and everybody tucked into them. Olivia couldn't help but hope that Hannah didn't tell Andrew about their meeting before thinking, *Stop thinking about it, Olivia – enough now!*

"I can't help looking at Anna's dress," Evelin began. "And need to visit your showroom."

"Yes, you do," said Olivia. "A little shopping therapy is a must."

"Yes, you're right. I'll look in my diary and text you some dates."

Olivia kept drinking glass after glass of champagne, feeling the need to really unwind. Her friends encouraged her to carry on, claiming she never relaxed. Well, there was her meditation, her yoga classes and her walks with Duke but to an extent they were right – she was very work oriented, which took a lot out of her. For a good hour, Andrew spoke about his new project – a hedge fund – and how excited he was about it. For some reason, Olivia felt bored and kept drinking.

Towards the end of the evening, Anna went outside to take a phone call. Evelin went to the bathroom and sitting next to Olivia, Andrew asked if she was all right.

"You seem far away from here tonight. Is something bothering you?"

"No, I'm fine," she said. "Maybe a little tired but it's the end of the week after all."

"You've been so supportive of me," said Andrew, taking her hand in his. "Let me drop you back home tonight. I know you're not driving, having been drinking."

Before Olivia could answer, Anna approached the table. "My new date has just called – the one I mentioned to you earlier." She looked at Andrew. "I met him on the plane."

"Oh, really? Well, you look excited. Is it finally somebody special?"

"I don't know yet, but I really like him," said Anna. "He makes me laugh and I feel myself around him. You'll like him too." She quaffed what remained of her drink and looked at Olivia. "Do you mind if Evelin or Andrew takes you home? I

84

have to leave soon, as I'm meeting Richard for a drink. He lives somewhere in Surrey too."

"I don't mind," answered Olivia. "It's nice to see you excited like that. Go and have some fun – I'll be fine with Evelin and Andrew.

Anna left like a shot after telling them to give Evelin a hug from her and that she would see her at the gym. Olivia was smiling and looked so relaxed. A few extra drinks really worked their magic on her and she noticed that Andrew kept looking at her with a lovely, sweet smile. But she didn't mind at all and, for the first time in ages, didn't try and analyse everything, allowing her thoughts to flow naturally.

"Hasn't Anna finished her conversation yet?" asked Evelin upon her return.

"Yes, she did, but she already left," said Olivia.

"But why?"

"She met some guy on the plane when flying back from a business trip. She seems really enthusiastic about it and said to give you a hug and that she'll see you at the gym."

"Ah, nice – another love story and I'm the last person to find out! Is something wrong with me? Or maybe I don't see you all enough because it seems that I'm always missing out on stuff going on."

"Oh, you know, Anna," Olivia began. "She only met him recently. I only found out about it today myself."

"And I only knew about it a few minutes ago before she left in a hurry to meet him," said Andrew.

"Wasn't she supposed to drive you back home, Olivia?" asked Evelin.

"Yes, she was," Andrew interrupted. "But I'm taking her instead."

"Great," said Evelin. "I have to leave soon, as my little one doesn't want to go to bed tonight until I get home – she's determined to wait for me and doesn't want her daddy to read to her instead. Poor David!"

"How is David?" Andrew asked. "He's not jealous of us, I hope."

"Oh, yes, he is, but he doesn't like to go out. He finds it tiring after a long week at work. He travels a lot as well but he trusts me and you all. Maybe it's better this way. I call it our balance – he's out a lot due to his work and I sometimes go out at the weekend."

"Send him our love," said Andrew. "We don't see much of him, so maybe I'll contact him and have a drink one day after work."

"That would be nice – let me know when that happens." Smiled Evelin.

They all left the restaurant together. After Evelin made her own way home, Olivia sat in Andrew's car and started to choose a song from his library.

"It's still quite early," she said, checking the time. "Not quite half past ten."

"You're right," said Andrew. "I can come over and we can watch something together."

"Yes, that's a nice idea. We haven't done that for a long time and I have popcorn and some other nice goodies."

"Good old habits." Smiled Andrew. "You always have some healthy snacks – and unhealthy drinks!"

"Well, this is my balance!" She giggled before singing along to the tune playing on the car stereo.

When they arrived at her house, she asked Andrew if they could take Duke for a short walk before bed. Andrew said it would be his pleasure to walk such a special boy and the three of them wandered down the surrounding streets. With Duke happily running around and sniffing anything that took his fancy, Andrew moved closer to Olivia, embracing her.

Looking at Duke's tail wagging furiously as he took in more scents, she felt glad to be in such a calm, happy moment. Leaning into her and looking straight into her eyes, Andrew started to kiss Olivia. She didn't reject the kiss, hugging him back and kissing him back too. It was a crazy moment and they both kept passionately kissing.

They must have looked like a young, teenage couple who had just found love. Olivia's head was spinning and her heart was beating so fast. She was a little confused but didn't want to stop. Finally, they looked at each other and holding hands, walked back to the house. Both of them were speechless and Olivia felt that this was something they had waited for, for a very long time.

She knew she was tipsy, which put her in a dilemma. On the one hand, she wanted to get in the house, grab Andrew and kiss him passionately until morning but, on the other, wondered how much of a role alcohol played in her emotions. As soon as they were inside, Andrew grabbed her, passionately picking her up and carrying her into the living room.

"I know we need to talk," he said, putting her down on a sofa, where he sat next to her. "I've been waiting for this moment and finally it's here. I'm not totally sure if we both want the same thing but I want to believe it. I don't want to make a mistake and lose you either, though. Please say something."

Olivia looked deeply into his eyes and said, "I don't want this to be a mistake either. It was beautiful out there – a perfect moment. But I know I've had a lot to drink and am afraid that tomorrow morning might bring a different feeling. I think it's best if you leave." Andrew started kissing her again but this time Olivia rejected him. "Please – you have to leave."

She stood up, walked into the hall and opened the door for him. She could tell from his expression that Andrew knew he had made a huge mistake.

"Of course. I'm sorry," said a mournful-looking Andrew, who left.

Olivia was so destroyed, she started to cry. "This is all my fault." She began to reprimand herself. "Why did I drink so much? I've behaved so badly. How could I have done that to our friendship? I could've stopped him but didn't – I even encouraged him more. Hannah is right – I'm selfish." She was so upset, she cried herself to sleep and spent the entire night on the couch.

By the time she woke on Sunday, it was almost lunchtime. Her head was spinning and she had several messages on her phone but decided to ignore them and make a coffee. Sitting down with her drink the night before came back to her in fragments. Continuing to rebuke herself, she had to tell herself to stop thinking about it and punishing herself – what was important now was how she would handle the situation and sort this mess out.

Picking her phone up, she started to go through her messages. Four awaited her from Anna, Evelin, Andrew and Hannah. She was shocked to see that Hannah had been in touch and listened to her message first. Apologising for being so childish and selfish, she asked for forgiveness and Olivia was hugely relieved, knowing that what happened between them wasn't her fault. Hannah's anger and frustration had been responsible for that but Olivia felt she was to blame for the tension between her and Andrew.

Having resisted reading Andrew's texts and listening to his voicemail messages – all four of them – she knew she had to meet the situation head-on. After reading his messages, she realised that he was feeling the same as her. He knew he made a mistake too and wanted to talk her to make things right, so Olivia decided to call him.

"Hello, Olivia," he answered in a calm voice. "Please, listen to me before you say anything. Firstly, my huge apologies and I hope you can forgive me for last night. I knew you were tipsy and I should never have tried to step into something that both of us should have been equally aware of and happy to discuss beforehand. It was a wonderful moment – sorry, I have to say this – but a wrong one and I hope you can give me a chance to make it right. Our friendship is priceless and so deep and I respect and value it so much."

"I'm sorry too," said Olivia. "And should have stopped you. I was tipsy but still knew what was going on. We're equally guilty for what happened last night.

I really hope we can get over it and keep what we have – our friendship, close to our hearts. Maybe this had to happen so we realise what we have that our friendship is way stronger, more beautiful and real than a romantic relationship. Our friendship is forever."

"Yes, it is and I'll do anything in my power to respect and cherish it."

"This is wrong – we should meet and talk," said Olivia.

"That I would love," replied Andrew. "But I'm on the other side of Surrey at the moment and am at my sister's this weekend."

"Well, send my love to her and let's talk next week."

"Yes, let's," said Andrew. "I'm so happy that we managed to talk. I couldn't sleep at all last night."

"I didn't fare much better." Laughed a relieved Olivia. "Ending up on the couch all night! I love you, my best friend, and never forget that. I'll be there for you, no matter what."

"The same with me," Andrew responded. "Bye for now."

Putting her phone down, Olivia jumped for joy. Her fear of losing Andrew had totally vanished and she knew that their friendship would, indeed, last forever.

Chapter Five
When You Love What You Create, the Power of Your Talent Becomes Irreplaceable

Olivia's work in the company had been very successful. She only had a few collections under her belt but the reaction to them had been tremendous and sales had gone through the roof, making huge profits for the company. She knew that it took time to adapt and prove herself in a new environment but she had shown that she had what it took and her hard work had been immensely rewarding. And while her focus wasn't on rewards, the feeling of success was satisfying and contagious. She simply never stopped, demanding constant improvement from herself.

It was mid-week when she received an email from the CEO, Simon, asking if she would like to join him and a few other company employees on a very important charity evening. The invitation looked beautiful and the charity name drew her attention. It was a kids' foundation that the company had been supportive of, for many years.

For some unknown reason, Olivia remembered meeting the little girl in the hair salon and the card her mother, or guardian, had left behind. She seemed to remember the foster charity organisation having a similar name to that on the invitation, which saw her remove all of the business cards she had collected from the silver box on her desk. *It'll be great if I can find more out about little Olivia*, she thought.

Going through all of the cards, she couldn't find what she was looking for. "How strange, I definitely remember saving the card and thinking I had to find her and get in touch one day," she said to herself. "Maybe I misplaced it. I'll try to find out at the hair salon – maybe they have one there."

She sat back down at her computer and replied to the email.

Dear, Mr Frazer, thank you for the invitation. It will be my pleasure to join you for this amazing cause and event. In life, the best way to grow is by helping, inspiring and sharing virtues I have always held, dear.

Sending the email, Olivia looked at the clock on the wall and, grabbing a folder from the desk, rushed to the board meeting that was to begin around five minutes later.

Baptiste joined her in the lift and smiling widely. "I presume we're heading to the same place," he said. "I wonder what this is all about. We usually have these types of meetings at the end of a season. Oh, while it's in my head, are you coming to the charity event? Because if you do, I will too."

"Yes, I'm coming – I've just confirmed via email. It's such a great project and an amazing cause. I couldn't attend last year but won't miss this one. I might have to do some research and learn more about it. Maybe we can have a coffee and you can explain more about the structure of the charity?"

"That's a great idea – how about Friday morning? I usually come in early on Fridays."

"That's perfect, thank you," said Olivia.

They entered the boardroom and sat down. The room was half empty and quiet. *This seems like a small, selected meeting*, thought Olivia. The doors opened and Simon and Sarah entered the room looking happy and excited.

Kicking the meeting off, Simon glanced around the room and, with a smile, said, "I know you're all wondering what this meeting is about but we want to share some great news with you. Our brand has been so successful and popular over the last two years that I want to thank you all. We've recorded great profits and today, I want to discuss with you a step forward...a future expansion.

"I believe fashion has been taken by storm in countries like China and the UAE. Our brand is very popular globally but we must never stop producing the best and must grow continuously. To this end, I had a conversation with Sarah beforehand and we decided to place Olivia in charge of expanding the brand in some essential territories. I understand that it'll involve lots of traveling and dedicated time but we believe Olivia will be able to handle that. I only hope that she agrees to it, so...what do you think?"

Olivia felt a little stunned but thrilled at the same time. "I'm totally honoured and delightfully surprised. I'll do whatever it takes to bring the best results to the table. I presume this will take a little time but with Baptiste, as my creative partner, I think we can achieve fantastic results, no matter what."

Baptiste smiled at her and put his thumbs up.

"We want you to travel to Hong Kong and China to start with, as soon as possible," said Sarah.

"Of course, you'll plan and choose your schedule. We just want to ensure that our company is one of the first luxury brands to expand in these up-and-coming countries in fashion. It's great to know that you have Baptiste as a committed colleague and partner. We'll need both of your help and input and must maintain the excellence of our collections.

"As we always mention, we're here to help and support you at every step of the way, so don't think you're alone – you only need to ask if you want us to step in. But I think that, when it comes to Olivia, nothing scares her – she's just a force of nature." She smiled at Olivia. "Not that I want to flatter you but we really believe in you and your great talent." Stepping towards her, Sarah passed Olivia a large folder. "This is something for you to look at."

Everybody in the room stood and clapped and, for a second, Olivia didn't know what to do – this was a really pleasant surprise. She blushed a little and said loudly, "Thank you so much for believing in me and my creativity."

Returning to her office, Olivia sat down on the sofa next to her desk. She had been dreaming of travelling since she was a little girl. Her creative mind always took her around the world and she loved the idea of exploring different cultures and learning about new traditions and history. *Life is an amazing journey*, she thought. *We just don't embrace and love our life enough.*

Opening the folder that Sarah gave her, she saw that it had contained heaps of information. It was the master structure that The Delaney Brothers made as a template to follow. But before she had a chance to really get stuck into it, there was a knock on the door.

"Yes, come," she said.

Baptiste entered the room and smiled. "Don't panic, I don't have bottle of champagne with me – yet. I didn't know last time when we were celebrating, that something even bigger would come our way – isn't life full of surprises?"

"It sure is," said Olivia. "And if we get to trust our instinct and rely on it more, it's even better."

"We have so much to do now; when do they expect you to travel?" he asked.

"I don't know yet, but I expect to be sent on my first assignment within weeks. Certainly not before the charity gala, which is in ten days' time."

"Great, we can talk tomorrow about how we can create a plan that works for both of us."

"Of course. And I'll arrange a meeting with our team to let them know as well."

"Okay, let me know if you need me," said Baptiste, who then left the office.

The first opportunity to really think about her promotion, Olivia found it hard to believe things had worked out quite so well. *Is this real or am I dreaming?* She asked herself quietly. *My life never has a dull moment! I'll have to talk to my family and friends to let them know.*

With her intuitive superpower returning, she knew that the next chapter in her life would be dramatic and powerful. Driving back home, she reminded herself to look into the charity whose gala she would be attending. She really wanted to make an impression and do some good, but how she would go about it eluded her for the moment. Her mind was everywhere – in Hong Kong, China and Dubai – so she decided to try and relax, rather than focusing too heavily on the future.

She reached home and took Duke out immediately. "Hey, buddy," she said. "You're the most patient, loyal and greatest friend."

Duke agreed by nodding his head.

"Now, that's spooky," she said with a smile. "I know you're very smart, but sometimes I question if what we think about dogs only touches the surface of what you are and what you know and understand."

On the way back from their walk, Olivia popped into the local shop to buy some chocolate, which she never kept at home, owing to her chocoholic tendencies. Returning home, she decided to make a quick tuna salad before enjoying the chocolate she had just bought. She gave Duke his dinner, then sat down to eat hers, thinking, *What am I going to do with Duke when I have to start travelling abroad for work? My baby boy will miss me and I need to think about what I'll do with him. It's not fair to expect him to travel with me, so I'll have to organise a dog sitter who'll be happy to move in while I'm away.*

After making herself a fresh mint tea, Olivia walked with box of chocolates in hand into the TV area. She removed some books to make space for the tea and chocolates when a business card fell down on the floor. Picking it up, she had in her hands the card from the hair salon. "Ah, here you are!" She smiled. "I knew you were hiding somewhere."

Rushing to grab her laptop and entering the company details from the card, she awaited a response from her search engine. It wasn't the foundation whose gala she had been invited to but it had a similar name. Saving the details on her computer, she promised herself she would give them a call the following day.

Olivia went into great depth, reading about the foundation and what it was doing. It was an old British charity that catered for the homeless and foster children with branches all over the UK. *The work that these amazing companies are doing is priceless*, she thought. *We live in such a bubble that we detach ourselves from the real world.* "I can't believe how many children are in foster care," she said looking at Duke.

Olivia carried on reading into the night, feeling sad that so many children were without homes…and glad that the charity was doing so much to mitigate the situation with its amazing work. She found the name and details of the woman she spoke to in the salon, then went to bed with a heavy heart. The following morning, once she had completed her office routine, she called the foster charity foundation, immediately recognising the strong, deep voice on the other end of the line, which belonged to the woman from the salon.

"Hi, Nancy," Olivia began. "I'm Olivia and we met when you were with a little girl – also called Olivia – at the Gary Thomas salon. It was a while ago now – well over a year."

"Oh, yes – you were the lady Olivia couldn't stop talking about. When she told me your name was Olivia too, I didn't believe her."

"I've been wondering how she's doing?"

"She's fine," said Nancy. "She was in a hospital for a while and then we struggled to find a foster carer for her. I was very attached to her. She's such a smart, lovely girl."

"I remember her beautiful, charming personality. Is there any chance you can arrange a meeting? I'd love to see her."

"Why don't you come to our offices? We're a short walk away from the salon. This way, you can find out a little more about Olivia and at the same time we can see how we can arrange a little chat with her."

"That sounds great," said Olivia. "I can try to come over this afternoon."

She knew it would be difficult to manage but really wanted to try. To her surprise, Nancy said yes and they arranged a time to meet. As the call ended, Olivia's heart was beating so fast, it felt like she had been running a marathon. Her hands were shaking as well and she questioned why she was reacting this way. Curiously, she somehow felt connected to a little girl she had only met once. *Maybe there's a possibility that I can find out more about her and the foster programme. I'd love to help, if I can*, she thought.

To distract herself, she called Michael. "We need to arrange a meeting for early next week," she told him. "And it's important that everybody from our department attends as I need to update staff about the changes that'll be happening soon. How are we getting on with the appointments for the fabric shows?"

"All done and confirmed – I'll send the confirmations today," said Michael.

"That's great. I need the dates as I have a very tight schedule from next week onwards. We have to start to work on the inspiration boards as soon as possible. Please bring me all of the trend magazines for the last few seasons, as well as the new ones. I'll need the pantone colours too. I want our new collection to be very different from the last."

"No worries. I'll gather everything and it'll be with you before the end of the day."

"Thank you," said Olivia. "I'm out of the office for a late lunch but my phone is always on, in case anything crops up."

Leaving the building during her lunch break, Olivia decided to grab something to eat on the way to meeting Nancy. Walking instead of catching a cab, Olivia called Evelin for a little chat.

"Hello, Miss Taylor, how are you today?" Evelin answered in a happy voice.

"I'm fine," answered Olivia. "And you?"

"I've finally sat down for the first time since the morning. I've had school runs, house work, shopping – you name it. Is work going okay?"

"Everything's fine, though I'm in a little emotional situation right now."

"Ah, no, don't tell me – it's Andrew," guessed Evelin.

"No, not Andrew…gosh, I need to see him soon, though, or he might think I'm avoiding him."

"Why? Is there something we don't know?" asked Evelin.

Olivia realised she had verbally expressed a thought pertaining to the second half of her sentence, which only invited more questions and should have been kept to herself. "No, I haven't really been in touch since everything went back to normal with his life. Actually, I called about something else. Remember me telling you that I met this little girl at my hair salon a while ago? Her name's Olivia and she looked very much like I did when I was a child."

"I do remember, yes – what happened?"

"Nothing, but I just found the foster company that looks after her and have decided to go visit them. I'd love to see her and find out how she's doing."

"This is spooky," said Evelin. "Sounds like you're going to adopt her."

"I don't know really but I want to find more out about her and the company."

"Maybe I can help?" asked Evelin.

"Well, I'm not in a position to look after myself properly and, of course, I have Duke as well but, strangely, I'm drawn to the girl and the charity."

"I don't know what to say. Usually, things like this end up with an adoption but you're even making me curious now and I'd like to meet little Olivia too."

"Maybe we can go together to see her at some point," suggested Olivia. "I'm meeting Nancy from the foundation in about 30 minutes."

"You never cease to amaze me, Olivia," said Evelin.

"I know you're thinking I'm nuts but I'm not. Everything in life happens for a reason and, for me, meeting her at the salon and then finding the company's card isn't just a coincidence. I don't know where all of this will lead but I might be able to help them. I always wanted to do charity work and this foundation is just amazing."

"I'll support you if that's your wish, Olivia," said Evelin. "And I like the idea of supporting a foundation that helps children. Maybe I'll get involved as well."

"Thank you for understanding. Once I have more details, I'll let you know."

"Damn, right, you will!" Joked Evelin. "I'll call you to find out how your meeting went."

Olivia reached the charity's HQ as she was saying goodbye to Evelin. Entering a tall, well-maintained building with a revolving door entrance, Nancy awaited her.

"Hi, Olivia, you're just in time! Come with me."

Olivia followed her into a small, basic but cosy office.

"Would you like a tea?" Nancy asked.

"Yes, please. Milk, one sugar."

"No problem. I know you're probably interested to know where Olivia is and how she's doing. She's recently been fostered but due to our confidentiality policy, I can't go into any details. But I'm happy to talk to her foster parents to see if they're happy for you to write her letters for now and maybe eventually see her as well."

"I'm very happy to know she's in safe hands with a family. Can I ask that have they only taken her for a limited time? Or they are considering adopting her?"

"Only for a limited time for now, but we always hope that fosterers go on to adopt."

"I see," said Olivia. "Can you tell me a little about her?"

"Of course," Nancy replied. "Little Olivia has a tragic past. Both of her parents passed away in a dreadful car accident. After that, she was looked after by her auntie, who was her mum's sister for over two years. She was the only relative Olivia had. Unfortunately, her aunt was diagnosed with cancer and was hospitalised for over six months, so it became impossible to keep her.

"Our organisation offered to help and, with her permission, we took full responsibility for looking after Olivia and helping her find the right family. She was only four when her parents died, so struggles to remember them now. But she knows what happened to them and really loves her Aunt Elizabeth. It's such a shame she's not well enough to look after her."

For a few moments, Olivia had tears in her eyes. "What a sad situation. How a little child can handle; it is just beyond my comprehension. I'm so amazed how brave she is. Please try to talk to her foster parents, as I would very much like to see her. We had this nice connection and, to be honest, I was shocked how much we looked alike.

"Looking at her reminded me of my childhood. Not just her looks but her personality too. She was so like me in so many ways, which is bizarre…though I don't believe in coincidences – everything happens for a reason and we just need to pay attention to it."

"I like your positive approach to life," said Nancy. "Let me see what I can do. If you leave some details with me, I'll be able to get in touch with you as soon as possible."

"That's very kind of you," said Olivia. "On another matter, our company has been very supportive of one of the biggest UK children's charities. I'd like to help if I can, so please send me details of how you work with companies and clients and what kind of help is most needed. All of my and the company's details are on my business card and I hope we can work together in the future."

Nancy escorted Olivia to the door and promised to get in touch soon. Walking back to her employer's, Olivia couldn't stop thinking about little Olivia, whispering to herself, *I wonder what the reason for me meeting little Olivia is? I'm sure I'll find out in time.*

Stopping at a coffee shop, she bought a hot chocolate. It was a little cold outside and she wanted to revive memories of her childhood. Her favourite drink growing up was hot chocolate and now her favourite desert was anything chocolate-based, so not much had changed!

Once back at The Delaney Brothers, Olivia went to see Baptiste. He was seriously focused on a screen when she entered the room, at which point he spun around in his chair to welcome her with a smile.

"Please, sit down, I want to show you something," he said.

She looked at the screen, saw a plethora of inspirational ideas on a board and figured he'd been brainstorming the inspiration board.

"I know how much time this takes, so thought that maybe we can work on it together."

"Why not? It's great to know you're already on the case. Why don't we stay until late today and put all of our ideas together? It'd be fantastic to have the theme and the inspiration completed before I leave. You can then start to work on the fabrics and designing the capsules."

"I'm in!" declared Baptiste. "I'll see you later then."

Olivia left and considered how lucky she was to have Baptiste as her partner, especially as they thought along the same lines. Entering her office, she found the trend books and previous collection catalogues on the floor, next to her desk. Michael was such a great personal assistant – what would she do without him? Then, literally a few seconds later, he entered the room with more stuff in his hands.

"Let me help you with that," said Olivia. "Can you sit down for a minute as I need to talk to you about something? It's confidential until next week Monday's meeting, when everybody else will know."

"I knew something was going on," said Michael as he sat down. "I hope it's a good news."

"Well, plenty of changes lie ahead for our department. From next month onwards, I'll be traveling a fair bit on behalf of the company, which wants to expand into Asia and the UAE. Baptiste will be in charge while I'm gone and I trust him because his discipline and style is fairly similar to mine. We're a great team and can achieve anything from anywhere in the world. You might have to travel too at some point, so please, bear that in mind. I'll give you the details once I have my schedule organised."

"Sounds good to me!" Smiled Michael, who looked happy with the probability of some travelling with Olivia.

"On another matter, I'll stay late today with Baptiste to start work on the inspiration boards. We have a theme already and you might have to stay as well."

"I'll be glad to help. I love it when we start work on a new collection!"

"I'll see you after 5 pm then," said Olivia. "Please continue what you were doing."

Olivia went back to her desk, wanting to meditate on the theme she had in mind for the collection. But then she thought, *No, I'll work on the collection with Baptiste, so will examine the files Sarah gave me instead.* She knew she needed to start planning her trip to Hong Kong and what to do while there and had to understand the market analysis regarding Asia and the UAE's main fashion trend and high-end shopping destinations. It was her intention to find gaps in the market that she could use to her and the company's advantage. These countries were so advanced in future fashion, technology and development and she had to know about everything that was fashion-related before she could plan her meetings in advance.

Looking over the file, she knew this a big responsibility and a huge step forward for the company. To be chosen and entrusted with such a big task was inspiring and evidence that she was good at her job. *I must deliver this project in the right manner, as there's no room for failure*, she thought. Olivia always expected more from herself, remembering one of her mantras; the higher you aim, the more you achieve.

Chapter Six
Finding Real Love Is Something We All Deserve

Olivia was on the way back to her hotel room after one of her business meetings. She rushed straight through the lobby and took the lift up to her floor, then entered her suite, a beautiful and luxurious apartment with amazing views.

It was late afternoon and just starting to get dark when she sat down and glanced at the room's desk, seeing a small pile of brochures and magazines from her previous meetings. *I left them there for a few days and now the pile is getting bigger, so I'd better have a look through them*, she thought. Standing up, she went to look at the pile of brochures when an envelope – glossy and in gold – attracted her attention. She opened the envelope and found a beautiful invitation card from Cosmopolitan magazine, which was celebrating an anniversary.

"This could be a good networking event for me," she said to herself. "A little social time is healthy therapy." The only thing was, the event was happening in two hours' time, that evening…but that wouldn't stop her. She took a quick shower and in no time rummaged through her wardrobe to choose a beautiful white structured dress, adding a light white coat. After a quick look at herself in the mirror, she applied some lipstick and left the hotel.

Outside a limousine, which came as part of her invitation, was waiting for her. Sitting in a luxurious leather seat, she thought, *Here we go, Olivia. Relax and have a great time. The only thing missing right now are my dear friends, Andrew, Anna and Evelin. I'll update them if something good happens.* Staring out of the window, Hong Kong at night looked magical. For a moment, she felt special, thanking her lucky stars for everything that had happened to her recently. *Life is beyond magical and special*, she thought. *We just never find time to appreciate and pay real attention to it.*

The car pulled up outside the venue, staging the event and Olivia became a touch nervous. A shy girl, she had never liked cameras. She had managed to practice a pose over the years, looking like she owned every place she attended but in reality, she preferred to take a back seat when it came to attention.

She stepped out, hearing her name being shouted by a crowd that had gathered outside while photographers' cameras flashed, amid calls for her to pose for them. Olivia waved and smiled at them, then walked into the venue, which was beautiful. She loved the manner in which Asian people designed venues, making a mental note to look into replicating such style. *They are so great with flowers and pastel colours*, she thought.

Walking into the middle of a majestic-looking room to look more closely at the flower designs, she bumped into a tall, handsome guy wearing a crisp black suit. "My apologies," she said, a little embarrassed. "I hope I haven't stepped on your shoes."

107

"Not to worry, you haven't," he said in a beautiful, posh English accent. "But you almost had my champagne all over your beautiful white dress."

She smiled and introduced herself, "I'm Olivia!"

He smiled and did likewise. "I'm Damian." He turned and took a glass of champagne from the tray next to him, offering it to Olivia.

"Thank you," said Olivia, thinking, *What a gentleman.*

"The pleasure is mine." Smiled Damian with his perfect voice and accent.

Olivia blushed for a second, not knowing why, as men didn't normally make her feel bashful. At that exact moment, Rene Young, the design director of Cosmopolitan Hong Kong made a beeline for her.

"I'm so pleased that you managed to come, darling Olivia," she said.

"Thank you for the invitation," said Olivia, as Rene wearing a striking cobalt blue, off the shoulder dress and smiled at Damian.

"It's lovely to see you, Mr Carter. I had no idea that you knew each other but I'm afraid I'm going to have to steal her for a moment."

Taking Olivia by the hand before Damian had the chance to say anything, Rene walked with her to a large crowd. Olivia was introduced to an array of very influential people in fashion and luxury goods, enjoying conversations with most of them.

One of the gentlemen she spoke to, Li Jun, was very keen on her work, loving her style and collections. As a representative of a key luxury manufacturer in China, he kept her busy for most of the night. While Olivia had no doubt that he did indeed love her work, it was obvious that he had a crash on her. Not wanting to hurt his feelings, she gave him her time – he was a lovely guy but not at all her type.

Towards midnight, Olivia looked at her watch and decided to head back to the hotel. She approached each of the people she met throughout the evening and said goodnight to all of them before Li Jun walked her to her limousine and helped her get in. Olivia thanked him for being such a gentleman, knowing she would probably never see him again unless it was business related.

On the way back to the hotel, she had such a happy feeling that she considered stopping the car to go for a walk but knew it was too late to do that in the middle of Hong Kong. *I'll go for a run tomorrow morning in the park next to the hotel instead*, she thought. *I haven't really done any exercise recently and, besides, it'll be great to see Hong Kong from a different dimension.*

She returned to the hotel and, tired, went straight to bed. Out of the blue, Damian popped into her head. "I wish I'd had the chance to speak to him a little more," she said quietly. "He was very attractive and his voice and accent were so sexy. Ah, well, never mind – I haven't the time for a man at the moment. You have a great mission to accomplish here, Olivia, so this is what you should think about."

Just before 6 am, she awoke, unable to get back to sleep. Remembering that she'd planned to go for a run the previous night, she had a good stretch, made an expresso, checked her emails and then went to the wardrobe to find her sports outfit, which she donned. Leaving the hotel at around 6.30 am, the sun was coming up and Olivia felt so happy that she had decided to go out for a run. *I should've done this every day since arriving*, she thought.

The park was hilly and had lots of steps but Olivia was curious to reach the top and see the view from up there. Clearing the final step, she came to a wide, open area with beautifully manicured trees and bushes. The view was amazing too, enabling her to see the centre of Hong Kong with its giant skyscrapers and modern architecture.

She had in front of her a long running path that led somewhere. "What a lovely surprise," she said to herself. "I love Hong Kong!" Starting to run again, Olivia looked at her Apple watch for a split second to see if it was recording how many steps she had taken when she bumped into somebody and fell down, feeling water splashing all over her. Looking up, she was pleasantly surprised to see Damian standing in front of her. "I'm so sorry," she said embarrassingly. "I can't believe I've bumped into you twice in 24 hours!" She could sense that he was happy to see her as she was him.

"Unfortunately, I couldn't save you from not getting wet this time," he jested. "I only stopped to have a sip of water when you disrupted my privacy – I hope you're not stalking me!"

Olivia blushed again – hell, he had a habit of reddening her face. "Oh, yes, your highness – I can't live without you. I even like to get wet at seven in the morning just to see you."

Damian helped her up. "You have a very cheeky character, don't you? Are you okay to carry on running?"

"That depends – are you asking me to join you?"

"Yes, I am, if you don't mind."

They both smiled and started to jog together.

"If we keep running this way, I'll show you something in about two to three minutes. You'll like it – it's a special view."

"Sounds great. I felt that when I reached the top, there was more to see in this park and I can't believe I haven't explored it earlier."

"You're not local, so what brought you to Hong Kong?" enquired Damian.

"I'm on business. What about you? You don't seem local either, with such an English accent."

"As a matter of fact, I am local – I live here most of the time. My accent comes from the UK because I grew up and was educated there. London is my second home."

"Lucky you, having to share these amazing worlds," said Olivia.

"What about you?" Damian asked. "Do you live in London?"

"I leave just outside London in Surrey," said Olivia. "I'm a country girl but I do work in London."

"Let me guess what do you do for a living – it must be something related to fashion or the media, as you were so warmly welcomed at last night's event. In fact, I couldn't even approach you – you were guarded like a Queen by a ring of admirers."

Olivia smiled and said proudly, "I'm a fashion designer for a global company and I'm here to see how we can expand our brand. Hong Kong and Asia in general are the key fashion destinations at the moment. We need to open more stores or see how we can get in direct contact with our consumers online."

"Impressive! I like your passion for what you do. Are you always like that?"

"Mostly. If I like something, then, yes, but if I don't, then I don't bother."

They carried on running a while before Damian stopped. "Close your eyes. Trust me – I won't disappoint you."

Olivia closed her eyes and was a little hesitant to walk but Damian gently took hold of her hand and started to tread slowly in a different direction. Olivia felt like a little girl playing hide and seek but she liked holding his hand. She felt secure and trusted him and inadvertently emitted a little chuckle.

"Is everything okay?" he asked.

"Yes, everything's fine. It's just that I don't know you, but it seems like I do."

Damian walked her a few steps forward, then said, "Open your eyes now."

Olivia opened her eyes and was totally amazed at the sight before her. A 360 degrees view, it looked like she had Hong Kong in the palm of her hand. From beautiful water views to architectural buildings, it was just magical.

"I often stop here to take a break," Damian continued. "It looks and feels special."

"Oh, yes, it's indeed very special! Thank you for sharing this amazing view with me. I'm getting inspired…has anybody had a catwalk show here? It would be one of the most amazing shows ever! Nature, combined with a 360-degree view of beautiful Hong Kong – wow!"

Olivia felt as if she had been infused with enthusiasm that she had been endowed with one of the most amazing gifts in the world. She could see that Damian couldn't take his eyes off her, mesmerised by her passion and excitement.

"What else do you do apart from running in the morning?" he asked her.

"I love yoga and I sometimes play golf and tennis. And you?"

"I play golf quite often. Tennis too but running is my favourite. Do you want to run back as well?"

"Yes, of course. I loved that view and must return before I go back home."

"Are you leaving soon?" Damian asked, looking a little panicked.

"Not yet. I've got around a week left here."

Damian lost his smile, looking at Olivia. "May I ask you out for dinner?"

Olivia didn't know what to say or think. She was so excited, yet a little hesitant too.

"I know an amazing place in town that I know you'll like – it's special too."

"Are you trying to get me excited before I answer?" Smiled Olivia. "Yes, dinner sounds great," she decided.

"What about tonight?" asked Damian, who looked at her like a little boy wanting a positive answer.

"I don't have any plans for tonight, so, yes, why not?"

Olivia heard traces of nerves in her voice, as she hadn't had a date in such a long time.

Damian smiled and said, "I won't disappoint you, I promise. Where are you staying? I presume in the Mandarin, as the hotel is the closest to the park."

"Sounds like you've been stalking me, not the other way around! I'll meet you in reception at seven tonight. And now, I have to go, I'm afraid."

"See you tonight," said Damian, who waved at Olivia as she ran down the steps like a little girl.

What a morning! she thought, feeling Damian's eyes on her as she ran all the way back to the hotel. The energy between them was magnetic, yet innocent…but was it a fatal attraction or love at first sight?

Olivia went straight to her room, needing to return her focus to business, having lined up some meetings for later that day. But as she sat in the car taking her to her first meeting, her mind was still at the park with Damian. When she caught him looking at her, his eyes were so bright with a huge sparkle. *He's such a handsome man*, she thought. *A perfect version of a male that you can't resist. But I guarantee he'll get the message that not every woman is the same. I can handle a man like that.*

The driver distracted her by letting her know that they had arrived at her destination. She got out of the car and was walking towards a huge glass building when somebody called her name from a distance. "Oh, no," she said to herself. "Not now, of all times." She then turned to face Li Jun, thinking, *Is this city so small that you can bump into everybody at once?*

"What a surprise to see you again," he said. "Are you meeting somebody in this building?"

"Yes," said Olivia. "Are you heading this way too?"

He smiled and said, "Yes, one of our offices is here. Who are you meeting? I might know them."

"Mr Smith, the global fashion director of luxury goods in Hong Kong."

"Oh, Mr Smith? He's on the floor below us. Perhaps, if you don't mind, you can visit our offices too. I can introduce you to my father, who's a very connected man in the fashion luxury sector and he might be able to help you."

Olivia had a meeting immediately after but thought, *This is a great opportunity and a contact that could be very important.* She thanked him for the invitation and confirmed a time. He let her take the lift first and wished her a successful meeting. *He's a very nice and well-mannered young man*, she thought.

Mr Smith was waiting for her as she stepped out of the lift that took her to his floor. After introducing Olivia to his team and asking if she wanted a coffee, they sat down in his office, which had a great view of the water. Olivia opened her file and gave him a copy of her presentation, then started talking through her plans for expansion.

"I want to achieve great things in Hong Kong and China but firstly, we'll start with Hong Kong," she said with confidence.

Mr Smith looked at her and said, "You've done your homework very well. I like your innovative ideas and think they'll work. The luxury sector needs innovative concepts that can be adapted to the Hong Kong market and your proposal is simple, clear and easy to execute."

Olivia shook his hand and said, "I'm here to expand our brand in any possible way and am looking forward to working with you on this great adventure." With a nice smile, she left his office. As she had a little time before her meeting with Li Jun's father, she decided to make a phone call to Andrew. Since leaving the UK, she had barely kept in touch with her friends, so she wanted to put that right. The phone kept ringing but there was no answer. She took the lift to the floor above, thinking, *Well, it's better to attend a meeting early than late.*

The lift opened and she stepped out onto an amazing floor with a great modern interior. The reception looked like a five-star luxury hotel lobby rather than offices and she always appreciated a beautiful design. Approaching reception and introducing herself, she told the young lady manning it that she was due to meet Li Jun and his father, Mr Young. The receptionist immediately called Li Jun and informed him that Miss Taylor was waiting. Introducing herself as May, she escorted Olivia to Mr Young's office. Walking behind her, Olivia couldn't help but look at the stunning decor surrounding her.

Entering an expansive, high-ceilinged office, Li Jun was sitting on a sofa with a man who looked very much like him. Both standing to greet her, Olivia smiled at them and said, "I hope I haven't interrupted your meeting. I'm here a little earlier than scheduled."

"No, not at all," said the older gentleman. "I'm Li Way Young, Li Jun's father, and it's lovely to meet you. Li Jun mentioned you earlier. He's very impressed with your design, skill and creativity in general and thinks you're amazing." He looked at Li Jun, who blushed. "Please, take a seat, Miss Taylor."

"Thank you. It's lovely to meet you, Li Way, and to see you again, Li Jun."

"It's good to see you again too. How was your meeting with Mr Smith?" Li Jun asked.

"It went well, thank you for asking," said Olivia, sitting down.

Li Way sat down too as did his son. "What's your specific aim in regards to your company in Asia? Do you have a goal or a plan that I can have a look at?"

"Yes, in fact I have a copy with me now." Olivia looked in her bag and, removing a clear folder, looked through the documents contained therein, then handed him a brief copy of her plans.

He took the copy and had a quick flick through it. "If you don't mind, I'll read this in greater detail, then come back to you. But if you'd like to tell me more about it now, I have ten minutes before my next meeting."

Olivia looked at Li Jun and then turning to his father, started to explain in detail what she believed would be a great way to expand The Delaney Brothers' brand in Asia. Her main aim was the digital world and it was a very clever one. Mr Li Way listened carefully and kept nodding his head but was silent throughout. Olivia felt like she was passing an exam but was determined to stay on track and accomplish what she was there to do.

She believed that every company should target the technological world and try to adapt to it as much as possible. She knew that fashion, especially luxury fashion needed a grand trading, flagship store in every large city but that should be it, apart from the boutique retail entities, of course. The flagship stores would have to be focused on customer service by entertaining customers, giving them the feeling of belonging to a private club and offering them packages involving other brands and exclusive hotel offers. Attention to detail for the consumer was Olivia's main focus.

"If we do manage to offer such packages, then we should make a digital platform that can be advertised and bring people together from any corner of the world, at least four times a year for networking and shopping experiences with our brand," she went on. "I have so much in my mind to offer but know I'll have to narrow the list and ensure that what's delivered is absolutely on-point…and if certain offers don't work, then we can adapt other ideas. The first year will be a testing period as we see how the marketing is evolving and what the main interest of our consumers are. To add to it, we'll create an innovative small capsule in each country, linked with its culture and history." Summarising the rest of her plans, she concluded, "And that's it – my master plan in five minutes!"

Li Way looked at her, then taking time to answer and said, "I know what I'm about to say might be inappropriate but if you ever consider leaving your current employer and I'll gladly welcome you here with open arms. You're a genius and a passionate lady. I like your way of thinking – it's attractive, structured and straight to the point. You're a living wealth creation machine. I definitely like your plan and am happy to be a part of it if you'll allow me. We can arrange a meeting to brainstorm together with Mr Smith on Monday week. By then, I'll have some more information for you."

Olivia was so pleased that she decided to follow her instinct and meet Li Jun's father. She knew that she was within touching distance of confirming a potential jackpot deal and was delighted that he was impressed with her plan.

"What a beautiful compliment, Mr Young," said Olivia. "I feel flattered. Thank you for your kind honesty."

He stood up shaking her hand and said, "I can foresee a great business relationship between us." Turning to Li Jun, he continued, "You have great taste in women, my son!"

Olivia blushed again, not knowing what to say in response and before she knew it, Li Way bade her farewell and left the room. Olivia looked at Li Jun, who was also blushing. She felt a little uncomfortable but knew from the beginning that he liked her very much.

"Thank you so much for introducing me to your father. He's such a lovely man. You must be very proud, having a father that serves as a role model and a friend."

Li Jun nodded. "Yes, he's a special man and I'm very proud of him. It was my pleasure to introduce you to him. I suspected you'd have lots in common. You're both in the same business and have similar stamina and drive for it."

"You suspected correctly," said Olivia as she rose to her feet. "But I'm afraid I have to run to another meeting and will talk to you over the weekend."

"Okay, speak to you then," he responded, the pair shaking hands before Olivia left.

Leaving the floor, she still was amazed at the huge difference between this and the others in the building. Reaching the downstairs reception, she ordered a taxi to her next meeting. Her meeting would be held over lunch at one of the Michelin Chines restaurants downtown and she only had 15 minutes to get there.

Figuring she might be a little late, she texted the person she was due to meet to inform her, then remembered Damian. She thought about what she might wear and briefly considered doing some clothes shopping before reminding herself that she had enough outfits back at the hotel.

And, besides, what was all the fuss about? It was just a dinner date after all. The car stopped and Olivia couldn't believe that she was already at her destination. *What is this daydreaming?* she asked herself. *You should be getting ready for your meeting, not thinking about personal matters.* Paying the taxi driver, she rushed to the restaurant she was due to meet in and even from the outside could feel the classic glamour of its decor. Luxury in Hong Kong was on another level and entering the building, she looked at her watch – it was two minutes before her meeting time and she had made it there in time.

She knew Rene, the lady she was about to meet from their university days and as Olivia approached, she was on the phone, loudly arguing with somebody while the lady sitting next to her seemed oblivious to her, looking at a menu. A pretty woman with bobbed dark hair, Rene returned to Hong Kong once she had graduated but they had kept in touch and met whenever she visited London.

When Olivia was asked to travel to Hong Kong, the first person to come to mind was Rene, who worked for a fashion magazine. They worked in similar industries, were good friends and always helped and supported each other. Rene looked at her, smiled and then told the person she had been speaking to, "I have to go now. I'll call you later."

Standing, she welcomed Olivia loudly, "My darling friend, Olivia, allow me to introduce you to another darling friend of mine, Silvia. Silvia is one of the main editors of Vogue in Hong Kong and we've been friends since childhood."

"When I approached the table, I could see that you must be related or have known each other for long enough for her to tolerate Rene's long, loud phone calls!" Joked Olivia.

They all laughed. "Yes, that's me," said Rene. "Loud and proud, as we all know. Let me introduce you to the most delicious restaurant in Hong Kong."

"It looks amazing and I'm sure it'll taste great too," said Olivia.

"Why don't we order first? Then we can talk business," Rene suggested.

"Sounds great. And because you know the place so well, why don't you surprise me with the order?" said Olivia with a cheeky smile.

Rene looked at Silvia and said, "We do this all the time. If Olivia knows the restaurant, I let her choose the menu and if I know the place then I choose the menu. We have a similar taste in food, so it's never a problem."

"You can choose for me as well then," said Silvia.

In no time, Rene had the manager all over them, catering to their needs, as did restaurant staff.

"Rene, is there anybody in this city that you don't know?" Olivia asked her.

"Hardly anybody," she said smiling. "I even met your Damian Carter a few times. Tell me how you know him – is it from London?"

Olivia was a little surprised and wasn't sure what to say. Silvia interrupted and said, "Well, if you know him, can I meet him too? I'd love to get to know him."

Rene looked at Silvia and said, "From what I remember last night, the way they both looked at each other, you don't stand a chance."

"Look, that's enough," said Olivia. "I don't know him at all. I only met him a few minutes before you came over and took me away."

121

"Okay, this is getting even more interesting," said Rene. "You both looked like you've known each other for ages, smiling away and having a relaxed, cosy conversation."

"Wrong psychology," said Olivia. "Like I said, I don't know him." She wanted to tell them that she was having dinner with him later but thought that it might have been too much information and involve explaining the whole story. Instead, she looked at Rene and asked, "You said you know of him. So, who is he?"

"Who is he? Only the most wanted man in our high society! He's handsome, charismatic, intelligent, successful and very rich – the dream package for all high society girls in Hong Kong."

"Is he a player?" Olivia asked.

"No, not at all…and because of it, he's even more desirable."

At that point, the food started to arrive and Olivia so desperately wanted to change the subject…but these two girls were happy to continue talking about Damian.

"Some of the girls say he must be gay because they consider themselves so beautiful but he's just not interested," Rene continued.

"What is he doing in terms of a career?" asked a blushing Olivia. "Why did you invite him last night?"

"He has lots of businesses. Some of them are linked with fashion and technology. If there's a big party in town, everybody invites him. Apparently, he's this genius who converts every business he takes over into a platinum concern."

"Okay, enough now," said Olivia. "You're making this guy sound like a God."

"He seemed very normal to me. But what is amazing is this food – what flavour and taste! This is more orgasmic than this Damian guy!"

"You're absolutely right," said Olivia. "Delicious food and the best I've had so far in Hong Kong."

Rene smiled and said, "Yes – ten points to me! Hong Kong has lots of great restaurants but this is special for me."

"Yes, it must be very special to you because you spend half your monthly income here." Giggled Silvia.

"Really?" Olivia smiled.

"Sure," said Rene. "And you know what? I don't regret it. I love good food and because this is so much better than good, I love to indulge on a weekly basis."

The girls looked at each other and giggled. The lunch passed quickly and they discussed potential business, including what Vogue and Cosmopolitan were prepared to offer her company. So far, every meeting that Olivia had in Hong Kong ended with great vibes and huge potential for the brand and she left the restaurant satisfied with what she had achieved since her arrival. But there was one thing she couldn't stop thinking about and that was Damian Carter, the mystery man who everybody wanted.

She looked at her watch to find that it was almost 4 pm. She would be meeting him in just a few hours' time, when she would hopefully find some more out about him. Sitting on the sofa in her room, she closed her eyes for a minute. It had been a busy day and Olivia felt that she needed a little meditation. Unintentionally drifting off to sleep, the ring of her phone woke her up. "Thank you for calling me," she told Andrew. "I fell asleep on the couch."

"Hong Kong is sucking all of your energy." Laughed Andrew. "I don't remember you sleeping during the day. Is everything okay?"

"Yes, of course. I just had a late night and a very early morning."

"So, lack of sleep then – I get it. I thought I'd give you a call because I haven't really had a chance to talk since you left."

Olivia looked at the clock in front of her and panicked. "You're not going to believe it but I'll have to talk to you tomorrow. I have a meeting at seven and only have 30 minutes to get ready."

"That's fine, no problem," said Andrew. "In fact, now I'm glad to have woken you up!"

"Absolutely, Dad – thank you for taking care of me, even when I'm so far away."

Ending the call with them both laughing, Olivia took a shower, then started to get ready. Choosing a nice yellow dress to wear, she added a light smattering of make-up, then left the room. She looked so fresh and natural and her little nap was the tonic she needed. Leaving the elevator, she spotted Damian from far away…and every inch of him was perfection – so much so that she couldn't take her eyes off him, his smile and appearance so inviting.

"You look divine," he said to her, offering his hand.

She took his hand and, smiling, said, "You don't look too bad yourself!"

They walked to a beautiful luxury car, where Damian opened the door and helped her in.

"How was your day?" she asked as he started the car's engine.

"Very busy, as usual. But I have a great feeling that my day is getting better by the minute!"

Olivia smiled. "Are you always so charming?"

"To be honest, not really but somehow your presence brings this cheeky persona out of me that I don't recognise."

"That's a good sign," said Olivia. "And means you feel comfortable in my presence."

"Are you always full of wisdom and knowledge in psychology?"

"Yes to knowledge in psychology – it's one of my hobbies."

"So that means you can read me right now?" He smiled.

"Maybe," she said and they both laughed.

Damian drove somewhere downtown into an area, Olivia couldn't recognise. "We're here," he said, pulling up. "This is a special place to me. I've been coming here for dinner since I was a little boy. My father brought me once and I loved the food so much that I kept coming back. After all of these years, it's still here and it has the same owner."

Olivia felt so emotional. She wanted to touch his hand but said, "Thank you. I feel so honoured that you're sharing this special place with me."

He helped her out of the car and, for a second, squeezed her hand. She looked at him with her big eyes and felt so secure and happy. The minute they entered the restaurant, a lovely old man approached to give Damian a hug. They looked so happy to see each other and Damian immediately introduced Olivia to him.

"Mr Choy, this is Olivia."

"So lovely to meet you, Mr Choy," said Olivia, shaking his hand.

"The pleasure is mine," he said. "I can retire, now that I've had the chance to meet you."

She looked at Damian and blushed. A smiling Damian took her hand and started to follow Mr Choy, who went to the corner of the restaurant and stopped by a table.

"I presume you'll have your favourite table?"

"Yes, thank you," said Damian as Mr Choy departed.

Olivia and Damian sat down. The place was busy but cosy at the same time. Not far from them, a young man played a beautiful song on a piano. The place felt magical and Olivia sensed that she was the first girl he had brought here. Feeling special and relaxed, she had a remarkable evening. She and Damian sat for hours talking and giggling, exchanging so many stories, from childhood to university, to family.

They had such a great time that neither of them once looked at the clock. Throughout the evening, they kept looking at each other with real attraction and emotion. It was so special that Olivia just knew that Damian hadn't entered her life by accident. She knew he was the man she had always thought would be impossible to find or even exist. He was so much like her in so many ways that they complimented each other beautifully.

The restaurant emptied and even the staff were nowhere to be found with only the piano man in the restaurant, still playing.

Damian looked at her and said, "It's getting late. I should take Miss Taylor back to the hotel like a gentleman."

Olivia smiled and said, "Yes, you're right – it's time to go back." But deep inside, she wanted this moment to last forever.

In the restaurant's car park, he gently hugged her and looking deep into her eyes, passionately kissed her. Every cell in her body reacted to it and Olivia hugged and kissed him back. It was clear to both of them that they were falling madly in love and, on the drive back to the hotel, Damian held her hand so tightly, it was as if he was afraid to let her go. He was focused on driving with part of the journey passing in silence. Late night, empty road and two souls so happily in love, this was a moment that both of them would remember forever.

Parking outside the hotel, Damian helped Olivia out of the car, then gently touched her waist and kissed her on the forehead. She could feel how strongly he wanted to grab her and kiss her and while his eyes shone like that of a protective lion, he controlled himself and remained a gentleman.

Olivia stopped by the entry door and turning once more towards him, smiled gently, waved and said good night. Entering her room, she removed her heels, laid in bed and closed her eyes. She could still smell his cologne and feel his hand touching her waist. She touched her lips, still feeling the most amazing kiss that she had ever had.

Olivia was so happy and fulfilled, she couldn't find the right words to describe how she was feeling. What she finally did know, though, was what it felt like to discover true love.

Chapter Seven
Making Fundamental Decisions
Leads You to Where You Belong

It was early spring time and Olivia already had already stored her winter clothes. She happily went through her spring/summer wardrobe, a routine she implemented twice a year to maintain her clothing function. Before she left the room, she touched a scarf and, with a smile on her face, went into the living room. It was Damian's scarf, which he had left behind by mistake but she was glad that he had, for it was a daily reminder of him. It was a Sunday morning but, rather than lying in, she had set her alarm and got up early, taking Duke for a walk, glad to have her wardrobe sorted until the autumn, when she would restart the vetting process.

Olivia sat down on a couch and looked at the picture frame that was in front of her – the lovely gift that Damian gave her. She recalled the day she received it. Both of them had cuddled up on a chair in the park – the same park that they ran in. She had a cup of tea in her hands and, tasting it, realised it was cold, having made it a little while ago.

Olivia was a little nervous about to meet her friends for first time since leaving the UK. She had to talk to them about

128

Damian and introduce him in a week's time when he was due to arrive in London. They all knew about him but not in any great detail and Olivia had butterflies in her stomach, just thinking about him. She had booked a pub lunch – a traditional English Sunday roast – her mouth-watering picturing it. Having been away for a while, Olivia missed her home, friends and, of course, traditional English cuisine. Surrey had a great selection of country gourmet pubs, the most popular of which was called the Queen Victoria, which happened to be Olivia's favourite too.

The day was so bright and sunny that she decided to take Duke with her, especially as most of the country pubs were encouraging dog owners to bring their pets with them. *What an advantage living in the country!* she thought. She had missed Duke loads while her friends hadn't seen him for a while either. Wearing a pair of jeans and a shirt, she grabbed a blazer and her hunter boots by the door, then left the house with Duke. He was so happy, knowing that his mummy was taking him out again. Opening the boot of her car, Duke jumped in and sat on his mattress, which Olivia made for him, so that even when they went out, he could feel comfortable and secure. Scrolling through her music list, she found the right tune and drove off.

"The two amigos," she said, looking at a tail-wagging Duke in the rear-view mirror.

Olivia had such positive vibes that morning – being back home and meeting her dear friends, it was a perfect Sunday. She was singing away and Duke was trying to join her, howling with his head sitting back on his shoulders. Olivia found it hilarious, knowing she would remember the moment forever. Managing to park just by the pub's entrance, she opened the boot and Duke jumped out with such a happy face, as if smiling, his tail wagging so frantically that it looked like a rotator.

Andrew appeared behind her. "What a great idea, bringing Duke along. What a perfect day out!"

Olivia turned to him and giving him a kiss on his cheek, smiled. "Yes, I thought. Well, why not? On such a beautiful day, we can eat outside and Duke can see you all too."

Clearly excited to see him, Duke jumped around Andrew, who gave him a man hug and a kiss on his soft, long ears. They all went in the garden, where lots of people were having a relaxed lunch time with their dogs. Olivia spotted a long table and went straight to it.

"This is perfect," she said. "In case Evelin comes with little Francis and David. I invited her along and really hope she makes it."

"Yes, she's coming with the whole family," said Andrew. "I just spoke to her. They're running a little late but should be with us very soon. And where's Anna? She's usually on time. I'll go inside and see. I bet she's by the bar, talking to some strangers or someone she knows."

Olivia looked at Andrew and laughed. "That's probably right!"

She sat down and secured Duke's harness to the table. He was so inquisitive, wanting to go and meet all of the dogs in the garden. Olivia looked around and thought, *Surrey is so beautiful in spring.* She closed her eyes, enjoying the sun, then heard Anna's giggling from afar. She was such a positive girl and always brought a happy energy with her.

A minute or two later, Anna's laughter drew closer. Olivia stood up and gave her a huge hug. The girls were so happy to reunite after Olivia's trips to Hong Kong and Dubai, which had kept them apart for a few months.

"Next time, I'll come with you," said Anna. "This has been too long! We've all been missing you loads but you decided to come back when the weather's getting better." She looked at Duke. "Hey, buddy, you must be the happiest dog to have your loving mama back home." She leaned down and gave Duke a nice stroke. "Shall we order drinks and wait for Evelin?"

"Yes, that's probably the best option."

Anna looked so radiant and, taking Olivia's hand in hers, said, "I'm so happy for you. You're officially off the market. The great British fashion designer, Olivia Spencer Taylor, is totally in love. It can make the best, happiest headlines on the news!"

"Don't be ridiculous, I don't want any publicity!" Olivia said before they both giggled.

Francis skipped towards the table, wasting no time in hugging Duke. "I missed you, my big doggy."

Olivia hugged Francis and kissed her on the forehead. "Hello, Francis! Where's Mum and Dad?"

"Dad's parking and Mum's on the phone. I couldn't wait and came to see Duke."

"Brave girl," said Anna. "Come to Auntie Anna – she needs a kiss too."

Francis walked around the table and went to give Anna a kiss. From a distance, Olivia could hear Evelin saying how happy she was that all of her friends were gathered together. She and David were talking to Andrew and Anna went to join them. Olivia and Francis looked at each other and smiled. "We'll wait for them to come here," Olivia told her.

"A sunny spring Sunday," said Evelin, looking at Olivia. "Is this because of you? Did you bring this lovely weather from abroad?"

"Oh, yes, I made a special deal with the weather in the UK." Smiled Olivia. "The good news is that it'll last until September."

They all smiled and sat down. After ordering drinks and the special British Sunday roast, Olivia was bombarded with questions about Damian while they ate their meals. Anna was so enthusiastic and happy, believing that Olivia's love infected her in a positive way.

"I'm amazed how handsome he is," she told Olivia. "You usually go for brains."

"Oh, yes, now this guy apparently has it all," Evelin said, looking at Olivia with a happy face.

"I'm jealous," said Anna. "Not a dark jealousy but still jealousy. Myself and Andrew will have to team up and party until both of us land somewhere nice. What do you think, Andrew? Can you handle me?"

"I think I can, we can give it a try," he said and laughed.

"It's a deal then," Anna continued. "We can invite Damian one evening to show him London from a different perspective."

"Oh, no, no, no," Olivia interrupted. "He grew up here and knows London better than any of us."

"Yes, I understand but he doesn't know it our way. And we need to get to know him alone anyway."

David stood next to Olivia. "Congratulations on your newfound love! You and Damian should come around for dinner one evening. I'll cook a nice, traditional meal for him."

"Thank you, David. Of course, we'll come by. He's very much looking forward to meeting you all. I've told him so much about you all."

Evelin moved close to Olivia. "David, move next to Francis, will you? When the meal comes, Francis prefers daddy next to her and, besides, I need to have a little catch-up."

Evelin sat down and, looking at Olivia, said, "Well, who could've guessed that you'd go abroad on business and return totally in love and beyond happy?"

"I love everything that life surprises us with," said Olivia. "You see, the happier you are, the more you attract positivity in life."

"That's for sure," Evelin agreed smiling. "We just need you around more often to remind us. I have a little news regarding little Olivia, by the way. I didn't want to talk to you on the phone. When you left, you asked if I could keep in touch with Nancy and see how we could find more out about Olivia and her foster family.

"Well, Nancy finally persuaded her foster family to let us visit her if we wish. She told Olivia about you and that you'd like to see her. Since then, Olivia has been drawing fashion dresses and is very much looking forward to seeing you when you can find time. I know you're very busy but this is great news as you were so keen to find her."

"Oh, good gracious," Olivia began. "I'm speechless! You're an angel! Thank you for not giving up. Can we arrange to visit little Olivia as soon as possible?"

"Of course. She lives in Kent with a nice family. They have another two foster children, who seem very nice and are happy to let you visit her. I'll talk to Nancy first thing in the morning to see what we can arrange for next week. I've spoken to the family, by the way. They wanted to find more out about you."

"I hope you haven't told them everything about me!" Olivia smiled.

"Not everything but important stuff that people like to hear," said Evelin. "Like your character and personality and your interest in maybe being able to help at some point."

"I can't explain how I feel right now," replied Olivia. "Being so busy and traveling abroad, so many things have changed and I've detached myself a little from my own life. You've just reminded me that it's time to get back to my real life. I can't wait to see that cute little face, which somehow reminds me of my childhood. You'll love her – she's just a little angel with a huge personality."

"Oh, yes, I can't wait either! Her foster parents have told me similar things about her."

"What are you talking about with such enthusiasm?" Andrew interrupted. "It looks like you're both up to something."

"Yes, we are, but not what you might think," said Evelin. "I'll let Olivia explain to you."

"What is it that you need to explain?" asked Anna. "I could hear your conversation from where I was standing."

"Okay," Olivia began, "a while ago, I met this little girl at the hairdresser's. She's a foster kid who looks like I did at her age and her name's Olivia too."

"That's spooky," said Anna.

"Yes, it is, but that's not all. Before I left for Hong Kong, I asked Evelin to help me get in touch with her. It's a long story but she just told me that I can see her soon. I'm very excited – she's a special girl."

"Are you considering adoption?" asked Andrew. "I thought you were in love and other things are more important?"

"No, no adoption…for now at least," said Olivia. "I just want to help. It'll be great to become a patron or ambassador for a great foster foundation like that. Helping children is something I always wanted to do but I wasn't sure in which capacity."

"Well done," said Andrew. "I'm a little confused…so only you and Evelin knew about this?"

"Yes, it happened just before I left. I didn't really have time to explain to you all. Sorry, it's not a big deal but little Olivia is a big deal to me. She's adorable and you'll all love her. If I get to meet her, then I can introduce you all to her too."

"That's not the most attractive news for me," said Anna. "I love children but only for a short period of time."

"Of course, darling. You're a child yourself. We understand your view towards children," said Evelin as everyone laughed.

"Thank you, I am a big child." Smiled Anna, who pulled a funny, naughty face, looking at Francis.

"But we're here to discuss our schedule for next week," said Olivia, changing the subject. "I want to make sure that everything goes to plan. Damian will only be here for a few days and it's important for me to know that we're all on the same page with the dinner in London."

"Yes, we are," said Anna. "You can't even imagine how much we're looking forward to meeting him."

"Don't worry, we'll make you proud and, from what we know already, he's Mr Charming," said Andrew.

"Okay, guys, please stop. He's a normal human being and I want you all to act normal."

Evelin touched Olivia's shoulder and, looking into her eyes, said, "Don't worry, everything will be great. We'll act normally. We're all adults here."

Olivia looked at all of them and said, "Thank you! What would I do without you all? I love you guys so much."

"And we love you back," said Anna.

It was getting a little cold outside and Evelin was ready to leave. "We have to go as I left our little one with my mother in-law. She has some stuff going on this afternoon."

"We had such a nice catch-up," said Andrew. "It was great to see you all."

"Agreed!" Smiled Anna.

They all waved to each other and went their separate ways. Olivia went straight home as she had so much to do, including catching-up with work. Having only been back a week, she had grabbed a stack of folders from her office to look at over the weekend and spent the rest of the day going through the collection that she and Baptiste worked on. Olivia had to review the summary she made for the board meeting coming up on Monday – all of the information summarising what she did in Hong Kong and Dubai. She opened a huge folder and started to leaf through it, page by page.

A good few hours passed until she removed herself from the folder. By then, it was late evening and she fancied a snack. Olivia went to the kitchen but going through her cupboards, realised she didn't have anything exciting to snack on, so grabbed Duke and a coat and left the house. On the way to the local news store, she stopped, leaving Duke to enjoy sniffing and walking around when her phone rang. Looking at the phone, her face lit-up – it was Damian.

My whole body has this amazing reaction when he calls, she thought. *The sensation is indescribable. I feel an amazing boost of energy exploding out of my chest and my mind becomes present and very sharp. It's like another level of my being is awakening and I feel like a superhuman. What's the meaning behind this great reaction? It must be that the love emotion is so strong.*

"Hi, Damian!" she answered in a radiant voice. "We must be telepathic – I was thinking of you when you called."

"I bet we are," Damian replied. "In fact, I think our combined energy is more than what any human has ever experienced."

Gosh, this is spooky, Olivia thought. *He sounds like me – is he feeling and experiencing the same emotions?*

"Are you there, Olivia?"

"Yes, I am," she responded. "Sorry, my mind was elsewhere. Well, I have to say I had a great lunch with my dear friends and we made a little plan to guarantee we fit everything in while you're here. Everybody is very much looking forward to meeting you, including Duke!"

"The same from my side," said Damian. "I'm counting the days and miss you. Separation is not working well for us."

"You're right – it's not. At least when I left Hong Kong, you followed me to Dubai. We'll have to create a strategic plan that'll work well for both of us."

"Yes," he agreed. "I have something in mind. We'll discuss it once I'm there. I'll talk to you later. I have to go now as I have a very early meeting."

"Of course," said Olivia. "Big hug and talk later."

Looking at her watch, she just realised it was about 4 am in Hong Kong. Walking back home with Duke, she thought, *I love my home and everything that surrounds me. If Damian can join us, Duke, that'll be ideal.* Deep inside, though, she knew it would be more complicated than she wanted to admit to adapt a schedule that would work for both of them. Reaching home, Olivia left her snack for the next day and went to bed – she had an early morning and a busy week ahead to prepare for.

The next morning, she left the house at 6 am and headed into London. She wanted to get to the office early and prepare for her presentation to the board. While in the elevator, she bumped into Sarah.

"You're early today!" She smiled. "I'm looking forward so much to our board meeting today. You've achieved loads and I'm sure you have a great master plan ready."

"Yes, something like that," replied Olivia. "I'm a little nervous but excited at the same time."

"I bet you are. Don't forget, we're a family here. Anything that's impossible out there is possible inside here," she said smiling and left the elevator.

Olivia felt great excitement and loved being back on familiar ground. *It's time to plant some seeds in the ground and start to make the brand bigger and stronger*, she thought. Her appetite for success had kicked in, fuelled by her enthusiasm. She was ready for anything that came her way. It was like she needed a reminder of what her mission and focus were about. With Damian in her life, she had upgraded her happiness and love but downgraded her stamina for success and achievement. What she needed now was to find a balance between success and love.

Olivia sat down in her office and was deeply focused on her computer when her office phone rang. It was 8.30 am and Evelin was on the other end of the line.

"Guess what? I've great news for you! We can meet little Olivia this week on Saturday. I know Damian will be here, so do you want to rearrange it for next week?"

"No," said Olivia. "I've been waiting for this moment for too long. Damian will understand. Besides, it'll only be for a few hours and he's bound to have some meetings to attend and lots more going on."

"Okay, boss," said Evelin. "I'll confirm on Saturday morning. We'll drive to Kent, where she lives. Her foster parents will meet us there."

"Evelin, you're amazing – you just made my day! I have this huge board meeting in 30 minutes and I was a little nervous. But this has made me so excited!"

"I'm glad to know I've contributed positively to your busy schedule. Good luck in your meeting and speak to you later."

"Thank you, sweetie," said Olivia, ending the call. For a moment, she questioned herself – *Why is the idea of little Olivia so important to me and the attraction of seeing her even bigger?* She told herself to stop analysing every step in her life and to try and let it be, believing that life unfolded in the best way possible for those pursuing positivity. "Focus on the meeting for now," she told herself.

At that moment, Michael entered the room with a coffee and a huge smile. "You've been here since seven, I bet, knowing you and your strive for perfection."

Olivia smiled and said, "I think you know me better than I can imagine! Are you ready?"

"Oh, yes, I most certainly am! You bombarded my inbox this weekend and I've been working on the presentation nonstop."

"Great – we're a perfect team," she said, leaving the room with him.

Heading into the meeting, Olivia reminder herself that the biggest parts of her life and character were her drive, stamina and thirst for learning; her desire to achieve and a curiosity that took her to previously untrodden paths.

The board meeting was so intense with stacks of information to cover everything she had done over the last few months. The moment she took to the stage, she became so naturally engaged and passionate that no matter how small or large the audience was, she managed to get everybody focused and present. She had been told that, watching her, it was easy to believe that she assumed the guise of a superhuman, with powers that not everybody had.

Her natural ability to talk and make jokes at the right time was just perfect. Towards the end of the presentation, Baptiste took over to further explain the collection projects that they had worked on for China and the Middle-East. The meeting lasted a good four hours and, as it neared its conclusion, Sarah stepped forward to speak.

"Attention, everybody! We've broken a record today – this meeting has officially been the longest we've ever had. This is one of the most important business projects that the company has focused on and the results so far are exceptional. Doubtless, we'll have lots of different views and opinions. So, we'll take a break until next week when we'll study in depth the business plan and take any questions."

Everybody agreed and left the room. Olivia was on her way out when Sarah stopped her.

"You've been such an amazing member of our company. We think you deserve more, so feel free to talk to me if there are any financial interests you wish to pursue or anything else that adds to your personal life."

"Thank you, Sarah, that's very thoughtful. I'll let you know." She left the floor thinking how far she had come since starting to work for The Delaney Brothers. *Hard work always pays off*, she thought. *At the end of the day, we're all motivated by knowledge, success, achievement, love, power and money.*

Olivia had a busy week and couldn't believe how quickly it passed. She couldn't wait to finally see Damian again. On the day of his arrival, she wanted to surprise him and went to the airport. Olivia knew it was a little childish but that's who she was and he loved that side of her character. By the time evening arrived, she was sat in the coffee shop next to Arrivals, sipping a Latte and keeping her eyes on the incoming passengers.

Finally, she saw him from afar. She wanted to run straight up to him but then a man and a young lady approached him. Olivia didn't know what to do – should she go and greet him or see what happened next? Walking down the terminal, two large men escorted them out. Olivia felt so confused and a little naïve, being there at that time. Was she being childish? Damian intimidated her with what she presumed were his staff and bodyguards but she hadn't expected him to be like this; she liked him the way he was in Hong Kong and Dubai.

Olivia loved beautiful things and was attracted to success but not this way. She realised that maybe she didn't know him as well as she had hoped and that she should have done some research to discover more about him. She knew from her friend in Hong Kong that he came from a very wealthy background but had fallen in love with a smart, intelligent man who was down to earth, loved simple things and never fussed about anything.

She was driving back home when Damian called her. Olivia froze; she didn't know what to do – should she answer and act like nothing had happened or be honest and tell him what was on her mind? She decided to calm down and call him back when she was ready. At that moment, she was in far too much of an emotional state, which she knew she would have to overcome because she was to have dinner with him in a few hours' time. Reaching home, she went to take a shower – a long shower or walk always helped her meditate and think rationally.

"Olivia, this is your fault – he is who he is," she said to herself. "You should've tried to discover more about his life." She knew that if she had told him that she was going to pick him up, none of this would have happened. It was getting late and, finally, she picked her phone up and dialled his number.

Damian answered immediately in a panicked voice. "Hi, are you okay?"

"Yes, I'm sorry, I had something going on when you called," said Olivia. "Welcome to London."

Changing the subject. "How was your flight?"

"It was great, thank you for asking. I can't wait to see you," he answered without delay.

"And me you."

"Please, allow me to pick you up," Damian continued.

All of a sudden, Olivia pictured him in a fancy car with bodyguards and staff, replying, "That's very kind of you but I'm in London. I've had a long day at work and decided to meet you from here."

"Okay, that's fine. I'll pick you up from work then."

Olivia had to admit to herself that he was very persuasive. "Great, see you soon."

She closed her phone down and panicked – she had lied about her whereabouts and now needed to get to the office ASAP. Grabbing some fresh clothes, Olivia left the house in a hurry, reassured that Duke would be well looked after by his dog sitter. This wasn't how she imagined seeing Damian – everything was chaotic and there was an-hour-and-a-half, and counting, before they were due to meet, it was a Thursday evening and London was very busy.

After an hour of driving, Olivia reached the office and went straight to the bathroom to change and get ready. She wanted to be on time, sure that her little white lie was just a hurdle and would be forgotten once she saw him. She missed him so much and realised it was pointless to jump to conclusions.

Looking in the mirror, she smiled, then closed her eyes for a good minute and, after a little breath in and out, opened her eyes and left the bathroom. Olivia looked so beautiful in a fitted, structured blue dress, suiting a classic, effortless style.

Her phone rang and it was Damian. "See you shortly, I'm on my way," she answered in a calm voice.

143

She was glowing, the energy around her growing exponentially, knowing that she would finally see him again in a minute or two. Seeing Damian waiting for her in the lobby, she passed through security and walked towards him. She could see his eyes radiating and his smile was so inviting. He hugged her and kissed her on the cheek. Nothing mattered anymore. They left the building holding hands.

Damian escorted her to his car, a beautiful two door black Bentley and opening the door helped Olivia to get in. She sat down and looked at the stunning black and white interior, a classic and beautiful combination.

Immediately after starting the car, Damian gently touched her hand and said, "I know you like Chinese food, so I've arranged for us to eat at Hakkasan tonight. I remembered you mentioned the restaurant in one of our conversations."

"Great choice!" Olivia smiled. "I'm quite hungry."

The journey to the restaurant went smoothly with the traffic in London thin on the ground. Olivia had butterflies in her stomach and, looking at Damian, stroked his silky hair. He smiled like a little child, clearly enjoying her touch. Entering the restaurant, it was quite busy but before even approaching the desk, the gentleman behind it welcomed them with a lovely smile.

"Hello, Mr Carter! It's so delightful, having you both dining with us tonight. Miss Taylor, do you care to leave your scarf with us or are you happy to keep it?"

Olivia was surprised that her name was mentioned as well. "Thank you for asking but I'm happy to keep it," she told him.

After sitting down in a nice spot in the restaurant, Olivia ordered water and a glass of champagne and Damian a glass of white wine.

He looked at her with a loving smile and said, "How was your week? I presume you have lots of pressure, coming back from Hong Kong and Dubai with exciting proposals and important information. I bet they're all over you."

"Yes, they are indeed," said Olivia. "I haven't really slept properly since I came back. But it's nice to be back home with Duke, my close friends and my creative work." She paused for a moment, looking into his eyes. "The only thing that was missing was you, but now I have it all."

Concentrating his gaze, Damian responded, "I want you to remember this moment forever. You're so special and important in my life. We have to talk about how we're going to sort out our distance. We're two grown-up adults and I believe we're ready to get to the next chapter in our…"

At that exact moment, the waiter approached and interrupted them, asking if they were ready to order. Damian blushed a little and looking at Olivia, said, "Ladies first."

After ordering, Olivia didn't know what to do and how to change the subject. Excusing herself, she went to the bathroom and on her way back could see Damian talking on the phone but the moment she approached, he finished the conversation, put his phone down and looked at her.

"Look, if you're not ready to talk, that's fine – we can come back to it later. You seem a little nervous and distant…is there anything wrong?"

"Yes, I'm afraid there is," Olivia began. "I went to the airport today to surprise you but seeing all of your entourage, I felt a little intimidated and taken by surprise. I know your lifestyle is probably very different to mine but we had such a great, normal time in Hong Kong and Dubai."

"I understand what you mean," he said. "Believe me, I prefer and love normal life too. In fact, most of the time my life is normal, apart from some very important meetings. So I'm sorry to hear that you faced a situation like that. If I'd have known, I would've cancelled my airport meeting…and I definitely prefer you over anything else." He took her hand and, looking in her eyes, said, "I love you and I know you love me too."

Olivia felt like her heart was about to explode out of her chest. She loved him so much and hearing him reassure her was so sexy and attractive. She felt like grabbing him and passionately kissing him, but knew she had to resist being in a public place.

Damian flashed her a dazzling smile. "I know what you're thinking right now and I want exactly the same."

Olivia felt like a little girl who had been caught doing something naughty and blushed.

"Let's eat something and go for a walk after," he said squeezing her hand.

They had a silent, quick dinner, wanting to be close to each other, their love so strong and innocent. Then, leaving the restaurant, they walked down the street holding hands and behaving like two teenagers talking, laughing and pulling funny, silly expressions. At one stage, Damian stopped goofing around, looked at her with a serious expression and said, "Don't go home tonight…stay with me."

Olivia nodded, confirming yes. Her face looked innocent, yet naughty. Damian loved her innocence so much and couldn't help himself, grabbing her strongly and kissing her passionately. It was like nothing else existed in the world, apart from both of them.

146

The next morning Olivia woke up and, looking around, smiled. She was so happy, stretching under the white silky bed linens. Her beautiful silhouette looked sexy and powerful while her long caramel hair and tanned skin were in sharp contrast to the white linens. She looked like a goddess who had just awoken; a stunning natural beauty.

Olivia looked around for something to wear and grabbing Damian's shirt from the night before, went into the living room. She heard his voice, far down the corridor. Damian was in the office, wearing his dressing gown, looking out of a window and talking on the phone. She approached him slowly and cuddled him from behind. He turned, smiled and kissed her on the forehead. She smiled back and wanted to leave but he grabbed her and told whoever he'd been speaking to that he had to go.

He gently took her by the waist and sat her on the desk. His eyes were fired up with warm, crazy love. Olivia was trapped by his heavy body, looked at him and couldn't resist. She started to kiss him, Damian responded and they gently undressed each other. The love between them was undeniably powerful and magnetic. They made passionate love, which was so pure and natural.

They were inseparable for the entire Friday. Olivia had taken the day off work, sensing that this would happen. Eventually, towards late afternoon, she had to go to the office to pick her car up, go home to see Duke and get ready for the dinner out with her friends.

They would finally meet Damian that evening – a significant moment in her life. Damian had a meeting in town and she decided to drive to his place, rather than letting him pick her up from her house. She loved to be in control in everything she did including driving.

She had just entered Damian's flat when her phone rang.

"Hey, miss love," said Anna. "How was it last night? Did you manage to go to the airport?"

"The evening went amazingly well," said Olivia, sidestepping the question about the airport. "We had a lot to catch-up on. In fact, he spoke about us taking the next step but I managed to change the subject."

"Why?" asked Anna. "You feel complete with him, so what's the matter?"

"Maybe I'm not ready," said Olivia. "I don't know. Maybe it's just a little too soon."

"Okay, I understand, Miss Perfect. I just hope you remember that love doesn't knock on the door many times. Anyway, help me with what to wear tonight. I don't want to be too flashy or too plain. I need my expert to give me some advice please."

They both laughed.

"I love your honesty," Olivia said. "Okay, I'll help you on one condition: don't tell Damian all of our crazy stories."

"Why?" asked Anna. "Are you afraid he won't like you anymore?"

They both laughed again.

"You know that's not the case. It's just that when you tell a story, you make it so dramatic and I get embarrassed."

"I know and that's why I'll make sure he knows all of our crazy stories!"

"Okay, then I can't help you, you little rebel." Chuckled Olivia.

After finishing her conversation with Anna, Olivia spoke to Andrew. He had called earlier but she had been driving and couldn't answer. Confirming the venue in which they were to meet, she sat on the sofa, closed her eyes for a minute and remembered that she needed to talk to Damian about the following day. She had to leave early, her meeting with little Olivia was arranged and she wouldn't miss it for the world.

Entering the bathroom, she started to get ready. Damian hurried in a few moments later.

"Sorry for being absent for so long," he said.

Olivia gave him a kiss and a cuddle. "Seeing you apologetic and worried, it suits you – I find it sexy."

They got ready quickly and, looking at each other, left the flat. Departing the building's elevator, both of them looked glamorous and dressed to perfection, like Mr and Mrs Bond. On the other hand, Evelin and David had some drama on their way to London. On the A3, they had a flat tyre and David had to improvise to solve the problem, changing the tyre himself to avoid having to wait for the AA to come to the rescue.

Olivia met Anna and Andrew on the doorstep of the restaurant they were to dine in, arriving at the same time. After talking for around five minutes, they decided to go inside. It was a great, casual way of introducing Damian to them. By the time they all reached the table, Damian and Andrew were focused on a business conversation. Anna and Olivia were looking at the menu when Evelin and David finally arrived. After all of them were introduced, Anna raised a toast and said, "This is to Olivia, Damian and our great friendship!"

The evening went smoothly and quickly and everybody was happy, getting on well. Olivia felt so secure and complete, thinking, *You can't ask for more than the love of your life and your best friends being together in such harmony*. Looking at them having fun, she smiled contentedly and thinking, *Life is a beautiful and special gift to us*. David had relaxed a little too much, electing to take a taxi home after the tyre situation. He never normally drank but looked to be really enjoying his night out.

Evelin looked at Olivia and smiling, winked, saying quietly, "I think somebody is really taking his night seriously."

"Oh, yes," said Anna. "But you know what? It's nice to see a reverse situation – it's usually you who's the relaxed one."

"Yes, you're right – I'm happy for him," said Evelin.

"Leave the man alone!" Joked Damian, interrupting the girls' conversation. "I couldn't help overhearing what you're talking about."

A few seats away, David and Andrew were involved in a heated conversation that seemed impossible to distract them from, while Olivia and Evelin laughed as Anna asked whether Damian's male friends were single.

Damian looked at them and smiling, said, "As a matter of fact, I do have a bunch of friends who are single. As you probably know, I was single just a few months ago too until I met this precious, beautiful lady who stole my heart."

"Ah, this is so romantic," said Anna. "Well, bear in mind that your special and stunning girlfriend has a single female friend who's dreaming of a prince on a white stallion."

Even David and Andrew stopped talking at that and they all laughed loudly.

"Is Anna always funny like that?" Damian asked Olivia.

Olivia nodded. "Yes, Anna's our twenty-four-seven acting entertainment but she's actually serious about what she just said."

Damian looked at Anna and said, "You have to go to Hollywood as personalities like you should be famous. You'll achieve so much."

"That's so flattering." Grinned Anna. "Thank you, Damian. You're the only one appreciating my talent."

In one voice, Evelin and Olivia said, "That's not fair – we've been asking and encouraging you since college to consider an acting career!"

"Yes, you're both right," said Anna. "But Hollywood is something else!"

They all laughed loudly again. It was getting late and Olivia had a few more drinks. She was beyond happy but at the same time could feel herself getting a little tipsy. It was very rare for her to let her guard down and properly relax. When everybody was ready to leave, Evelin looked at Olivia and said, "Do you want to meet up in Kent tomorrow morning or would you prefer if we travelled there together?"

Realising she didn't have time to talk to Damian about it, Olivia looked at Evelin and said, "I'll text you later to confirm." Damian looked at her, confused, but Olivia smiled and said, "I'll explain to you on the way home."

They all said goodnight to each other and went their separate ways. Olivia walked to the car with Damian, who hugged her and placed his jacket over her shoulders.

She smiled and said, "Thank you, I'm a little cold."

They arrived at his place and Olivia went straight to the fridge to open a bottle of champagne.

151

Damian leaned on the kitchen door, watching her. "You're so attractive when you're tipsy. I hope you know that."

She looked at him and smiled, lifting the bottle in her hand. "I hope you don't mind. We had such a beautiful, relaxed evening and I want to continue the night like that."

"Great idea. I can join you as we have no responsibilities until morning," he said looking at her with a cheeky smile. "Besides, I bought that bottle for us for last night but we've been too busy."

She smiled back and said, "We can get busy again."

"Are you teasing me now?" said Damian, approaching her and kissing her on the neck while she was getting the glasses ready. He took the bottle out of her hands and said, "You go and relax in the living room. I'll bring it in and add some ice in a bucket to keep the bottle cold."

"Yes, captain," said Olivia, who smiled and left the room.

She sat on a sofa and relaxed with her feet up. She was tipsy and totally happy. Damian entered the room with a glass of champagne in his hand. Handing her the glass, he kissed her gently, disappeared into the kitchen and then returned with the rest of the champagne and some strawberries.

He sat next to her and asked, "What's happening tomorrow morning? Are you busy with work or something else?"

Olivia sat up straight and, for a moment, became serious. "Sorry, I forgot to mention that I have an important meeting tomorrow and Evelin is coming with me. It's a long story."

"Tell me," he insisted. "I want to know all about it."

"Well, a while ago, I met this little girl in the hairdresser's and she reminded me of myself when I was her age. Her name is Olivia too – can you believe it?" She looked at Damian, who was patiently listening to her. "Little did I know, she's a foster child. I always wanted to help children, especially homeless children. I didn't know where to start or what to do, but I followed my instinct and went to look for her. Evelin helped me find her and finally I'm meeting her tomorrow." Olivia's eyes were on fire when she spoke about little Olivia and her voice was so passionate. "Sorry for not mentioning this to you earlier. Are you okay? You haven't really said anything."

"I don't know what to say," Damian began. "I understand that you felt a connection with this child. But from the looks of it, you're going to get yourself into a very complicated situation. You're such a young, vibrant woman, capable of having your own children. I think maybe this isn't the right moment for you to make your life even more complicated."

Olivia was so confused but responded immediately. "I'm not adopting her, if that's what you're thinking. I want to help her; I don't know why but I want to know her more. She's such a beautiful angel. Why don't you come with us tomorrow? You can meet her too."

Damian moved a little from where he was sitting, looked at her sideways and said, "I'm sorry, I don't want to meet anybody at the moment. I don't think you're aware of the situation you're placing yourself in."

Olivia felt herself getting hot under the collar, then completely lost her temper. "How dare you talk to me like that – I'm not a child! I know exactly what I'm doing! This little girl needs somebody to support her and give her a chance. Clearly we're on different pages on this matter."

"I understand your sympathy and that you want to help her. But I know it'll get more complicated. I thought it was all about us and how we were going to progress our relationship together. This is a little too much for me, so why don't we just end the conversation?"

In Olivia's mind, she replayed him arriving at the airport and his lofty lifestyle. There was a man she wasn't familiar with and he was here too, with alcohol clearly not helping matters.

She stood up and said, "I'm sorry but I don't think our relationship stands a chance of progressing. I'm gutted at your reaction to a child that needs help!" Damian motioned to interrupt her but Olivia continued, "This is over! Sorry, but we're not compatible."

Damian looked taken aback. "Let's talk about it tomorrow. You had a little too much to drink. Let's not aggravate the situation."

Olivia shook her head in amazement. "That's amazing!" she exclaimed, thinking, *He thinks this is the alcohol, not me! He clearly doesn't know me and I don't know him.* Grabbing her coat and bag, she said, "I have to go. Our relationship was too beautiful to be real. Please, don't contact me."

And with that, she left. A stunned Damian didn't try and stop her and didn't even turn to look at her. Olivia walked to the car park, furious about what had just happened. Getting into her car, she quickly drove off. Angry and shocked, she put some music on loud as tears ran down her cheeks like a river.

It was gone midnight and the road was dead. She drove back home so quickly that she was back in Surrey in no time. After parking the car, she burst into tears. It was as if a big

154

part of her heart had been snatched away from her and she felt lost in her thoughts. She loved Damian so much, it was so painful to think even about it.

She entered the house and remembered that Duke was with her dog sitter. She had left him with her, knowing that her weekend would be busy with Damian. She wanted so much to cuddle Duke, her loyal loving buddy at that moment. Heading into the bathroom, she looked in the mirror to find her face covered in mascara. Taking her clothes off, she took a shower to try and calm down – this felt like a bad dream that was bearing down so heavily upon her chest that she couldn't breathe.

Olivia couldn't sleep that night, tormented by what had been a cruel turn of events. It was only as the clock ticked towards morning that she was able to grab a few minutes before her alarm woke her. Getting out of bed, she made for her coffee machine, remembering that she should have texted Evelin. She put that right without delay, finding her phone and sending Evelina a text to say that she was at home, ready for her to come by whenever it was convenient.

The morning passed so slowly – Olivia besieged by the images flashing through her mind. She was calmer but her chest was still in pain and her mind was too tired to digest anything. She didn't know what to say to Evelin and wanted to focus on little Olivia and redirect her thinking but it was too much. She wanted to scream with pain, anger, disappointment and confusion.

Her doorbell ringing, she opened the door and forced a smile. Evelin looked at her and was shocked. She knew something had happened because Olivia had no life in her and looked totally destroyed. Evelin hugged her and Olivia hugged her back. They sat by the door for almost a minute, hugging. Olivia had tears running down her face and didn't want to be the strong girl anymore.

They went into the lounge, where Evelin sat her down on a sofa. "Olivia, what on earth happened?"

"My fairy tale love is over!" Snivelled Olivia.

"It can't be over just like that. Come on, tell me what happened?"

"I told him about little Olivia and he reacted like a man who I don't want to know anymore. I walked out on him and made it clear that it was over."

"Why did you react like that?" asked Evelin. "Maybe he's one of these guys who needs time."

"I don't know why I reacted like that. The alcohol probably played a part but he didn't help either. It just happened and I can't go back or take back what I said to him. I know he's a very strong-willed, proud man. He'll never call or come back but after what happened, I can't call him or chase him. He was wrong to start with, regarding his opinion on little Olivia."

"Do you want me to cancel the meeting?" asked Evelin. "We don't have to go."

"No, we're going. Just give me a minute to put some makeup on. All of this happened because of this meeting but I want to see Olivia. I've been waiting for this moment."

"Okay then, let's go. We can talk on the way and I'll drive. Things can change and, knowing you and how strong you are, makes me feel better."

Olivia went to the bathroom and quickly put some makeup on before they left the house in a hurry. The journey to Kent was slow and the rain didn't help. Olivia told Evelin about the airport situation and that she saw a different Damian that day. She knew that was his business profile but it made her realise she needed more time to get to know him in greater depth. She kept reminding herself that her instinct never failed her. On the other hand, Evelin tried to balance the conversation and keep her positive.

"We only have a couple of miles to go," said Evelin. "Can you believe that in a few minutes, you'll see little Olivia? I've never met her but feel connected to her already."

"I understand what you mean – she has the same effect on me as well. You'll fall in love with her. I know that for a fact. Don't react too spookily – she looks identical to me when I was her age."

They finally arrived at the address. Olivia walked down the path leading to the house and pressed the doorbell. Her heart was beating fast with excitement and she took Evelin's hand and squeezed it. The door opened and there stood little Olivia. Her beautiful eyes were so happy and her smile was so innocent. Behind her was her foster parent, a tall, middle-aged woman.

Evelin looked dumbfounded at the resemblance between the two Olivias, who were practically identical. Little Olivia ran to Olivia and hugged her. Olivia dropped to her knees and hugged her back. She closed her eyes and, for a moment, nothing mattered anymore – she didn't have any pain, anger or hate. She felt safe, calm and a huge burst of innocent, pure love. A love that was emotional and powerful in equal measures.

Chapter Eight
Inspiration and Imagination
Are the Core Value of Creativity

A few months passed by since Olivia and Damian split up. Since then, neither of them made the effort to try and fix the situation. They were equally stubborn, strongly opinionated and proud personalities, which was a pity as they made such a great couple and so much passion had passed between them.

And so, without Damian in her life, Olivia dedicated her life to work, friends and little Liv. Little Olivia had asked her to be called Liv, since everybody she knew addressed her that way. Olivia loved the name Liv – a shortened version of Olivia – which worked well for both of them.

She had donated a great amount of her savings to the Foster Foundation that Liv was a part of and, visiting her on a weekly basis, their friendship became so strong that they were virtually inseparable. Olivia inspired little Liv, teaching her how to draw and create and design little capsules for her dolls.

Life was moving on but her heart was still bleeding in silence. Her love for Damian was the strongest she'd ever had for a man. She lost weight and looked unhealthy and her smile only shone when she was on her way to meet Liv. Her friends and everybody around her started to worry and for good reason; she didn't look great and didn't feel great either.

Unbeknown to Olivia, a concerned Andrew had called Evelin and Anna, telling them they needed to come up with a plan to ease her pain. Anna suggested a call to Damian, whose phone number and email address she was in possession of, though Andrew and Evelin were opposed to the idea, knowing how Olivia would react and that she might never forgive Anna for calling him.

"We all know Olivia too well," said Andrew. "We can't make mistakes, so let's find the right strategy to really lift her spirits and get her appetite for life back."

"How about a holiday?" Evelin suggested. "She needs to go away for a while and we could join her too."

"That's a great idea," said Anna. "She loves yoga and meditation, so maybe we can organise a break somewhere in Tibet or India."

"I think Thailand might be better. It's a beautiful country and has more Westernised parts as well. She needs to be in an environment that'll uplift her. If Olivia ends up in Tibet, she'll come back as a monk. Whereas in Thailand, she can relax and meditate and if she fancies going out to explore, she'll have a bigger choice. Besides, I know she'll love Phuket and some of the other islands there."

"Well, it sounds like our plan is almost there." Smiled Evelin. "Let's look online at the packages. We can meet her this week and send her away over the weekend. And if all goes according to plan, we can join her too. But if she's fine on her own, we'll leave her to it."

"I can research and find the best package for her," said Anna. "I know you're busy with your family, Evelin and I like to negotiate and get the best out of a package."

"Please allow me to cover the payment," said Andrew. "It's the least I can do for her."

"I'll arrange drinks for us and maybe a dinner on Thursday," said Evelin. "We can send her away on Saturday or Sunday."

"What about her job?" asked Anna, a little panicked.

"Ah, don't worry about it. She's been working more than anybody put together in that company. I'm sure they're aware that something isn't right with her either."

"Yes, you're right," said Anna. "She'll have Friday to sort it out. It'll be fine…"

They all loved and approved the perfect idea. Standing by the side of the road, waiting for a black cab, Andrew looked at his watch. He was on his way to a meeting but was pleased that Olivia would soon be on a plane to sunnier climes.

He cared about her a lot and had felt useless, being unable to help her, having distanced herself from the world with only work and Liv mattering to her. They all understood and gave her space but seeing her sinking was so sad and painful. She deserved the best, this amazing, hardworking woman, who dedicated her time to other people, rather than herself. A break would do her the world of good, help her reflect on life a little and bring her closer to the light at the end of the tunnel.

Olivia was at work when Evelin called her. Her phone was on silent but she held it in her hand, about to make a call. "Hi, sweetie," she answered without hesitation. "How are you?"

"I'm fine, thank you for asking. We're all fine. How are you and how's work?"

"The same, all fine too," said Olivia. "I'm sorry I haven't really kept in touch with you all recently. It's such a busy time at work."

"That's fine, no worries," Evelin responded. "It's nice to hear your voice, at least. I was going through some of our photographs last night and thought to myself that I'm going to call you today and try to arrange a coffee, lunch or even dinner. What do you think?"

"I don't know if I fancy going out, but a lunch sounds great! How about coming to my place on Saturday?"

"Sounds good but I have the feeling you're avoiding all of us. We love and care about you. Why don't we have dinner on Thursday? Maybe Anna and Andrew can join us. We can go somewhere local, not far from home."

Olivia felt a little guilty, knowing she had let her friends down by finding excuses not to meet. "Okay, Thursday evening's fine. I'm sorry for being so distant. I just needed some time on my own. But you're right – I can't keep going on like this. If you can ask Anna and Andrew to come, that'll be nice. But do book something local – I don't want to dine in London at the moment."

"Consider it done," said Evelin. "We all miss you. It'll be lovely to have a low-key dinner."

"Great," said Olivia in a happier voice. "I have to go now – I'm just wrapping something up before going home. It's nice to hear your voice too. See you soon."

Sitting on the sofa next to her desk, looking at a framed photograph of her with her friends, she smiled, then finished her day's work. Time went by so quickly and on Thursday morning, while she was in the elevator on her way up to a meeting, she received a message with the details about the dinner. Closing her phone, she looked at the mirror in the elevator, smiled and left the floor.

Her meeting was with Sarah and before entering her office, Olivia asked her PA for a coffee.

"Hi, Olivia!" Sarah exclaimed, smiling widely. "Guess what? Today at 6 am, I became a grandmother. I'm just so happy! Would you like to see our little grandson, a magical baby boy? His name's Valentine."

"Oh, of course!" Grinned Olivia. Looking at a picture of the baby, she could see how proud Sarah was of the little bundle of joy and could feel positive energy exuding from her. "He's so adorable and has your eyes and smile. Oh, how I love babies!"

"Thanks, Olivia! You might be asking yourself why I asked you to come and see me. You're such an amazing person, Olivia, and a total workaholic. But I fear your health and self-esteem might need a break. You've dedicated so much time to the company and we all appreciate your great efforts and achievements. Don't forget, we're like a big family here."

"I don't know what to say," Olivia began. "But, thank you. I probably could do with a break. I'm seeing my closest friends tonight for dinner and thinking about them has made me realise I haven't kept in touch with them. You're right: I'm a workaholic but I love what I do and that's why I can easily get into the extremes of it. Maybe I should take next week off. Let me think about it and I'll confirm in an email to you."

"That's fine. I just want you to be happy and healthy," said Sarah. "I miss seeing that big smile on your face and your great sense of humour, which lightens the heart of every employee. A good holiday's a great idea and I need one too. Since you started working with us, you haven't had a break. I'm taking my holiday next month, so I can spend more time with our daughter and our little grandchild."

After Sarah hugged her, Olivia walked out of her office, thinking, *Everybody around me is caring and wants me to be happy. I've made myself such a victim after my split from Damian and need to get back to my old self. I'm so happy that my dear friends have arranged dinner tonight. I'll make an effort and dress up – I'll surprise them!*

Smiling, Olivia left work early so that she could go home and get ready for dinner. Texting Evelin to inform her that she would see them all at the restaurant within an hour, she was ready to exit the house. She looked so beautiful, wearing a smart, casual pair of leather trousers and a boxy blouse. She always loved electric or bold colours as an accent and her bag and shoes were electric lime green with black. Her makeup and hair was simple and fresh and even she was impressed when glancing at her reflection in a mirror before leaving the house.

Andrew, Anna and Evelin were already at the restaurant, having decided to meet up ten minutes before Olivia was due to arrive in order to ensure their plan was going accordingly.

"I think you, Andrew, should open the conversation about our plan. This was your idea, and Olivia always listens to you more carefully than us," said Evelin.

"That's fine," said Andrew. "I'm happy to do that." He looked at the girls, smiled and nodded at the entry door.

Olivia entered the restaurant and they were all surprised. She looked so beautiful and, for the first time in a while, had a smile on her face. Approaching the table they were sat around, Olivia kissed each of them.

"Did I make a mistake? Am I on time? Usually, I'm the first one to arrive, but tonight I'm the last."

"No," said Anna, kissing Olivia on the cheek. "We got here a little early – surprise!"

"This is great!" Giggled Olivia. "Thank you for organising this and for coming together. I want to apologise for not keeping in touch and for being distant. I promise I'll never do it again. I miss you all and love you dearly. Please forgive me."

Andrew looked at Olivia and said, "We left you to it, purely because we felt that you needed to be alone for a while. Sometimes, we need to figure out sensitive situations in silence. We all handle our situations differently but we knew that it was time to put an end to it. So, a dinner was ideal to bring all of us together like the olden days."

"You look beautiful," said Anna. "It's nice to see you've made an effort. How's Duke handling you?"

"He's been my best buddy. He's so adorable! He brings most of his toys next to the sofa in the living room and talks to me in a craving way, forcing me to play with him."

"That's my buddy!" Laughed Andrew.

"How are you all?" asked Olivia, looking at them all. "Please, tell me you're all fine and no huge changes have occurred since I disappeared."

"We're all fine," said Evelin. "Just getting on with things, so no news from our side. How's little Liv? We hope she kept you entertained in our absence."

"Liv's fine!" Beamed Olivia. "We have such a strong friendship. Maybe we should all have a picnic one weekend."

"That sounds great," said Anna. "We can have a big, fat picnic!"

"Like a big, fat, Greek wedding, you mean!" Quipped Olivia, all of them laughing. "Let's start from now – I fancy some champagne!"

In no time, Andrew ordered a bottle, which was brought to their table. Raising a glass of bubbly, he said, "We have something for you as a gift. We've thought carefully about your situation and came to the conclusion that you need a break – a holiday. You might try to cancel and say no but tough! Everything's arranged and booked already." He handed Olivia an envelope. "Please, you have to accept our gift and, if you really want to make us happy, so we can forgive you, you'll go on that holiday."

"You didn't have to do this," said a touched Olivia. "You all have your own lives with priorities like family and work. I don't know what to say. Thank you but it's a little too much."

"Olivia, darling, you've done lots of great stuff for us over the years," said Evelin. "And besides, you are our family. We thought of everything in detail, so you'd better open that envelope and see what's in there. We're so excited to see if we got this right!"

Olivia opened the envelope and with a huge smile on her face, looked at the destination they'd chosen for her. "This is exactly the type of holiday I'd organise for myself! You all definitely know me way too well! This is amazing – today, our Managing Director, Sarah, made me realise I need a break and I promised her I'll take a holiday from Monday.

"This is too coincidental," she went on, wondering whether they had colluded with Sarah to synchronise the time she would be off work. Looking at her friends, she started to well-up, tears cascading down her face. "This is such a great gift! Thank you for your great support and for organising the trip. I'll be on the plane on Sunday, I promise. Today has been such a special day, which shifted my energy and I won't be going back into my shell. I love you all."

Smiling, she stood up and went to give them all a hug. She was a great believer in human power and the impact it can have on people. She loved spreading love, hugs and taking the positive vibes out of any situation. A proud optimist, she called herself.

The dinner went beautifully and her friends were so happy to see her smiling and making jokes. After a few hours of this special night, they all went home.

Olivia entered the house and could hear how excited Duke was, waiting by the door. Fussing over him as she entered the house, she made her way to the kitchen, opening the garden door and going outside with him.

It was a full moon out and the garden looked magical. Sitting on a bench, breathing in and out, Olivia felt hugely relieved, her body feeling lighter as if a weight had been lifted from her shoulders, enabling her to think clearly. Her quantum energy field was so strong that she could feel it around her. It felt like an awakening that a negative energy had just left her for good.

Stepping back indoors, Olivia grabbed her laptop and sent a quick email to Sarah, letting her know that she had considered her idea of a holiday and that she would be away for two weeks. Heading upstairs, she started to prepare her packing. Her meticulous approach took time but in the end her luggage looked like a work of art itself. Her perfection never failed her and she was proud of it.

Visiting little Liv on Saturday, they had a great time colouring some fashion illustrations and talking about how industry collections were made. Olivia explained that she would be away for two weeks but that when she got back, she would arrange a picnic for them to enjoy with her friends. Liv liked the idea and Olivia promised she would call her while away and bring her a nice gift from Thailand.

It was Sunday morning, the day she was leaving for her holiday. After a quick meditation, the fact that she needed a break became even clearer and that her positive energy needed sustaining. Her inspiration and creativity had been lacking recently while her personal life was a mess. She knew that only she could change the direction her life was taking and she was determined to do it. She felt so lucky to have such great friends and was grateful for the amazing holiday they had arranged for her.

Once she was on the plane, an air hostess welcomed her aboard, offering her a glass of champagne.

"I'm Natalie." She smiled. "I'm a good friend of Anna's and a great fan of your designs. Anna loves you so much and I'll do everything I can to make sure you have the best trip today."

"Thank you," said Olivia, sitting down while smiling at Natalie. "I'm very much looking forward to it."

Settling into a nice first-class seat, she sensed something under her legs, standing to find a note – from her friends, wishing her a fabulous time – she hadn't noticed when sitting down. She was so happy and somehow felt that they were there with her for a second. Looking out of the window, she felt something special...that the trip would have a huge impact on her life...that something was about to change...but

167

what? She couldn't help but smile and looked forward to arriving in Phuket.

The flight was great and Natalie kept spoiling her with champagne and treats like Belgium chocolate. There was no opening of emails pertaining to The Delaney Brothers, Olivia deciding that anything work-related would have to wait unless absolutely essential. She wanted to really focus on exploring Thailand, once she was there, as well as relaxing and practicing a deeper meditation.

To help pass the time, she read a biography she had recently purchased and found it so gripping that she had practically finished it by the time the plane landed. On her way off the flight, she approached Natalie and gave her a notebook that she had designed for the brand.

"Oh, thank you so much," said Natalie, Olivia waving her goodbye, glad to have put another smile on another face.

She arrived at the Amanpuri Hotel and, shortly after checking-in, decided to go and explore the resort. It was such a calm, secluded place and the view from her bedroom, looking out at the turquoise Andaman Sea was magical. *I can't believe I'll be spending my two weeks in this amazing, special place*, she thought.

Olivia grabbed her hat and was ready to go out for a walk when she bumped into her butler at the door. Relatively short in stature, he was dressed smartly and had neatly coiffured dark hair.

"Hello, Madam Taylor, my name is Sanun. I'll be your butler for the rest of your trip. Please don't hesitate to ask for anything. I'm very happy to help."

Olivia smiled and said, "Nice to meet you, Sanun. Thank you in advance for your help. I'll try to remember your name – it's a weakness of mine!"

He looked at her and smiling, said, "You can call me, Happy, if that makes it easier. My name in English means happy."

"I like that – what a beautiful meaning! But I'll try to remember your Thai name. I want to explore a little of the resort. How can I get to the beach?"

Sanun gave her a map and explained clearly how to get there. He offered to take her to the beach as well but Olivia wanted to find it on her own…and, indeed, she had a great time exploring the resort. Finding the beach and taking her sandals off, she went for a walk. It was late afternoon, surprisingly quiet and really was a paradise.

Finding some large rocks on one side of the beach, she sat down. She appreciated even more what her friends had done for her, the holiday feeling more special by the minute. Feeling the time was right for a short meditation, she closed her eyes. The only movement she could hear was the sound of the waves and all she could feel was a light breeze on her body. She was calm and relaxed; her body and her mind were synchronised and the feeling was so magnetic and powerful. *I could stay here for the whole evening*, she thought.

After a while, Olivia opened her eyes and, looking at the endless sea and the beautiful golden sand, smiled, then started to head back to the resort. Entering her room, she sat on a chair next to a window, marvelling again at the sight before her. She looked at her phone, thinking that she might need to order room service when her phone rang. It was her dear friend, Andrew, calling.

"Andrew, I don't have enough words to describe this beautiful place." She gushed. "It's simply a paradise! I'm forever grateful for this amazing, dream holiday. You must allow me to pay you all back – it's too generous."

"I'm glad to hear the excitement in your voice. You deserve a treat. Please don't mention any paying back, as we did this from the bottom of our hearts. I knew you'd love Phuket. Amanpuri is very secluded but you have access to anything you want, from visiting temples, elephant riding, fantastic shows, shopping and other great beaches…the list is endless."

"I'm so happy being out here," Olivia responded. "I really needed a holiday. I suppose we don't realise what we miss until we take time to reflect. I haven't stopped since I started working. I have enough time to reflect on everything in my life now. By the way, I've had already a short meditation by the beach and it felt so special."

Andrew could hear the excitement in her voice. She sounded like a child who had been given something new to explore and he was so pleased to hear her being happy and positive. "I must admit, it took me, Evelin and Anna a while to come up with the best way of getting you out of your workaholic routine and make you remember yourself. I'll call Anna and Evelin to let them know that you're fine and happy. They'll probably talk to you tomorrow. I bet they can't wait to hear everything in detail! Sorry to cut this short but I'm at work, so I'll have to go. But speak again soon."

"Bye, Andrew." Olivia took a guide book from a desk and started to look through it. She thought of planning her week ahead, to ensure she managed to explore Phuket and the neighbouring islands as much as she could. Ordering room

170

service, she decided to dine in. She had only recently been on a long flight, so this seemed like the best option for her.

Opening her computer, she googled all of the temples around. *Buddhism has the best meditation retreats and temples*, she thought. *I always wanted to experience and learn more about meditation. This is just perfect – finally, I'll be able to achieve my goal.*

With a nice, fancy cocktail in her hand and a plate of sushi, Olivia sat on the terrace, watching some boats far away. The sunset was just mesmerising, leaving her speechless. For a minute, she remembered Damian and the time they spent in Dubai, watching the sunset together. She stood up and walking to the living room, switched the TV on, needing a distraction and started to flick through its film library.

There was no point in spoiling the day and, besides, she wasn't upset or angry with Damian. She had simply moved on and chose to remember the beautiful time she had with him. *Life is unpredictable and what we had was special. I'll always cherish my special moments in life*, she thought.

Olivia fell asleep on the sofa watching TV, something she never did at home. But it didn't matter – not everything in life was about discipline and even workaholics had to relax without obsessing over what came next.

The following morning, Olivia opened her eyes and checked her watch to find it was 5 am. Wriggling out of bed, she stretched, then took a bottle of water from the table, walking out onto the terrace. In the corner was a yoga matt, which she unrolled to stretch out on. It was a perfect way to start the day; meditation while looking at the endless sea.

Asking Sanun for a bowl of fruit for her breakfast, she decided to dedicate the holiday to her body and mind. Then,

171

shortly after 8 am, she walked to the reception and ordered a car for the day, so that she could visit a few temples and maybe some other sights. Climbing into the passenger seat, her driver greeted her with a beaming smile.

"Good morning, Miss Taylor, my name is Tom and I'm very happy to assist you today. I was born in Phuket, so am well-placed to advise as to tourist destinations."

"That's very kind of you, thank you," said Olivia. "I'm more interested in your local communities, culture, temples, markets and beaches where the locals go. I want to have a feel of how the real Phuket people live, not the foreigners."

"I'm speechless, Miss Taylor. You're one of very few who wants to see the real lifestyle of a local Thai. I'll do my best."

That morning alone, they visited two temples and met a few monks. Tom seemed to know lots of people and introduced Olivia to them. He was a proud Thai man and that was reflected in his character. While talking to some of his friends, they suggested some other temples, away from Phuket, that were very secluded. Olivia loved the idea of visiting places that were more private and naturally kept.

For her late lunch, Tom took her to a nice Thai restaurant. She could see that it belonged to a family with even the youngest member – no more than around ten years old – on hand to help. The food was delicious and the hospitality was just amazing. Olivia couldn't help but observe that the Thai culture was very welcoming, happy and humble.

Towards late evening, after practically the entire day sightseeing, she walked back to her room with a fabric bag full of little gifts and books. She felt so lucky and grateful, meeting so many friendly people and visiting such amazing temples. She was overwhelmed with joy and had acquired so much knowledge in a matter of hours. Tom had been such a good driver that she booked him for the following day as well.

Olivia placed the bag next to the desk in the living room, grabbed a book from the bag, and went straight for a swim in the pool. After a few lengths, she got out, dried herself and went into the lounge, where she sat down and opened the book. Looking old with plenty of use, it was a meditation book that one of the monks had given her as a gift. He was so impressed with her knowledge of meditation that he felt the need to give her one of his own books, which a Tibetan monk had bestowed upon him while traveling.

She was totally captivated by the book, only the sound of the doorbell distracting her. Walking back inside, she remembered she hadn't had dinner yet. And when she answered the door, it was Sanun, who had in his hands a bowl full of fresh fruit.

"I didn't want to replace the fruits for you during the day, knowing that you'd be out." He smiled. "But now that you are back, I thought you might enjoy some of our local produce."

The bowl certainly looked colourful with pomelo, passion fruit and other beautiful fruits.

"You must've read my mind," said Olivia. "I was thinking that I haven't really had a dinner but having had a late lunch, I don't really feel hungry. The fruits are just perfect!"

"Oh, Miss Taylor, this is not good enough. You must have something more substantial too. If you don't mind, I'll bring you a nice Thai soup called *Tom Yam*. It's light and filling, and I promise you'll like it. You may have had it before but our chef makes a very special one. Please allow me to get you a bowl full."

173

"A bowl of soup sounds great," she said. "Thank you."

"What do you prefer – chicken or prawns?" asked Sanun.

"Prawns might be a better choice." She smiled.

"Good choice! I'll see you shortly," he said and left.

The next morning, Olivia woke up early again, wanting to maintain her yoga and meditation before she left for another long day. Placing some sweets she purchased at the airport in her shoulder bag, she left in a hurry, realising she was running late. Waiting for her in reception was Tom, who she left with after saying good morning to everybody there. Olivia had a nice feeling that today would be a wonderful, productive day like yesterday. And maybe even special.

The weather was amazing and, glancing outside, she promised to call Liv, wanting to know what she had been doing recently.

"Are you ready for today's adventure?" Tom asked, distracting her.

"Oh, yes," Olivia responded, looking at him. "Yesterday, you introduced me to some amazing places. I'll never forget them and will have to come back here so I can visit them again."

"We have a long way to go today but in between I'll stop at another special place – somewhere you'll like."

After a long drive, Tom went off the main road and through some backstreets. The road was bumpy and the houses were smaller and more typically Thai than those she had seen near the hotel. The surrounding streets had some children running around while adults sat in the shade by their houses. Olivia could see the sea line and realised Tom was taking her to the beach.

Pulling over to park, he said, "I'll walk with you for a while and show you something. Then, if you want, you can spend some time over there. I'll be watching you from a distance, though it's safe out here and quiet too."

Getting out of the car, Olivia glanced around, seeing a lovely forest festooned with palm trees to her right and then to her left some huts and beach restaurants.

Tom walked towards the trees, looked at her and said, "We have a little walking to do but I don't think you'll mind once we reach the place I'm talking about."

Olivia smiled and followed him. They kept walking for about five minutes until they reached a stunningly beautiful, private, secluded beach, which looked like something from a postcard.

"We've arrived!" Tom declared, smiling. "Feel free to stay as long as you want. I'll stay here in the shade."

Olivia smiled back at him and walked towards the water. Taking her shoes off and putting them in her bag, the sand was warm under her feet. Removing her camera from the bag, she took some pictures and kept walking, stunned by the enveloping scenery. On one side was a beautiful turquoise sea and on the other beautiful palm trees with white sand sandwiched between them.

Turning around, she glanced back to see if she could still see Tom. He was far away and the more she walked, the more her curiosity encouraged her to go forward. Reaching a curve and looking forward, she could see some nice palms close to the water and a few rocks. Deciding to sit there and meditate, the beach was empty. *What a beautiful place, yet nobody's here to enjoy it*, she thought.

Olivia felt like a child at heart, wanting to jump in the sea, run on the sand and scream with happiness. Carefully placing her bag on the rocks, she found her scarf in her bag, laying it out on the sand next to the beautiful curved palms standing at the water's edge. Sitting down, she took a succession of huge breaths in and out, looking at the sea. Closing her eyes and placing her hands on her knees, she wanted to memorise the scene so that it stuck in her mind forever and promised to picture it while meditating at home.

For a few minutes, she was so deep into her meditation that time seemed to stop until, out of the blue, a group of children ran towards the sea, talking and laughing loudly. Behind them was a quiet, short man who walked a baby elephant towards the water. Olivia couldn't believe what she was seeing – another great, no filter postcard.

The children were half naked and looked like street kids with more boys than girls. Looking towards Olivia, they realised they were not alone and then, once the elephant reached the water, they rushed towards it and started to splash it with water. The lovely baby elephant loved it, swinging its trunk about as if returning the gesture. Olivia managed to get some pictures and was completely mesmerised by what was unfolding before her eyes.

She was totally drawn to the elephant and children and started to head towards them. Smiling and greeting them in Thai, the children replied and moved nearer to her. Getting a closer look, Olivia noticed that their clothes and faces were dirty despite having been in the sea and that the clothes had holes in them. Beautiful smiles adorned those faces, their eyes full of curiosity and excitement.

She looked at the man and asked him if she could stroke the elephant. The man didn't really understand English but smiled and nodded. Olivia stepped towards the baby elephant and started to stroke it. It kept turning and looking at her, touching her with its trunk. She was in such a happy state like she was in the middle of a dream she didn't want to end. The kids started to splash her with water and she smiled and splashed them back.

The man told them off but the kids looked at him and giggled. Remembering that she had some sweets in her bag, Olivia offered them to the children. They all grabbed at the sweets and said something to her, probably thanking her before she heard Tom calling her name. Turning around, she saw him walking towards them.

"Just checking you're okay, Miss Taylor?" he asked.

"I'm totally fine," said Olivia. "I've made some new friends here, as you can see!"

One of the girls ran towards where Olivia was sitting, took the scarf from the beach and started dancing with it, some of the other kids following her. Olivia smiled and watched them, then turned towards Tom and said, "Can you please say thank you to this lovely man for letting me intrude upon their privacy."

Tom looked at the man and told him something. The man replied, smiling and gesturing towards the children.

"These children are orphans," Tom told her. "They live in an orphanage close by and he wanted to make them happy, bringing the baby elephant to them." Olivia knew something wasn't right when she saw their clothes and the dirt on them. She felt sad for a moment and turned towards the children to see where they were. They all sat down on her scarf, making some sand figures with sticks.

She approached them and opened her bag, which contained some hair bands and another scarf. She looked at the girls and, taking her hairbrush from the bag, started to brush their hair, which she made ponytails out of and other styles. They were all so happy and curious, studying her. An older boy approached and give her a hug. Olivia smiled and hugged them all.

"You're so kind and special, Miss Taylor." Smiled Tom. "You've made their day."

"Thank you for bringing me here," she said. "I think they've made my day too."

The man stepped over to Tom, asking him something.

"Miss Taylor, I hope I'm not being rude asking you this, but what's your work back home? This man thinks you're a teacher."

"I'm a fashion designer," she said without hesitation. "I make clothes."

Tom looked at the man and relayed what she had said to him. All of a sudden, the children all came closer to her, one of them starting to draw something in the sand. The girl who had taken her scarf wrapped herself in it, making a dress out of it. A smiling Olivia made it look better, then some of the other children grabbed her hand and led her towards the boy drawing something.

She looked at the drawing and couldn't believe her eyes – he had depicted a sketch of a girl dressed up and even made some nice designs on the dress. Marvelling at their creative skill, she opened her phone, sat down next to them and showed them her designs. They all were amazed, looking

178

carefully at the pictures. One little girl stood up and started to draw her own figure, which was as good as the boy's. She looked at Olivia and told her, in broken English, that the figure on the sand was her. Olivia smiled and gave her a hug, wanting to find more out about them and to spend more time with them.

"Tom, please find out where the orphanage is, as I would like to visit them before I leave."

"If that's what you want, I'll find out," he said. "But we must go now."

Olivia smiled at the children once more and responded, "That's fine, we can leave now but only if you promise you'll find the orphanage for me."

"I promise," said Tom.

Olivia approached the man and said, "Tom, please can you translate. I want to give you some money, so you can buy lunch for all of these lovely children. I trust you because I can see how generous you are, visiting them with your baby elephant. I know you'll get them a nice lunch at one of these local restaurants."

Olivia gave the man some money and hugged him. He was in tears and kept saying, "Thank you." She left the beach with such a happy feeling, yet was a little sad at the same time. She kept looking back at them, seeing the children playing with the baby elephant, running and jumping. Free in this world, but happy, despite not having parents to guide them and give them security and love.

Olivia had a busy day visiting the local, smaller islands, another temple and some other places. Arriving back at the resort, she went straight back to the hotel. Her mind was with the lovely children she met earlier in the day and little Olivia too.

The world is such an unfair place. Nobody deserves to grow up like that and I want to do something that'll inspire and help them, she thought to herself. After a shower and wearing some fresh clothes, she stepped onto the terrace and decided to call Liv. There was no answer the first time she called, but trying again a few minutes later, Liv answered. Olivia nearly leapt up with joy, asking, "Hi, Liv, how are you?"

"I'm well, thank you," Liv replied. "I've been waiting for your call."

"I'm sorry for not calling you earlier. But I'm here now, so tell me what have you been doing recently?"

"Oh, nothing new – school, homework…I've been drawing too and think I have an idea for your new collection. You remember you asked me to think about it? I'll explain once you get back. How's Thailand? Is it beautiful and warm out there?"

"Yes, it is," said Olivia. "I met some nice children today and they're talented like you. They love drawing in the sand. I miss you, Liv, and promise you'll have a nice present from Thailand when I see you again. I'm sure you'll like it."

"What is it?" she asked. "No, don't tell me – I like surprises," she added with a giggle.

After few more minutes of talking, Olivia said goodbye to Liv and ended the call. Her face was sad – she missed that little girl so much already – so she opened her yoga mat and sat in a meditation pose. Her mind was too busy thinking about too many things at once, a short meditation was in order to balance her busy mind. While trying to calm down and focus on her breathing, Olivia relaxed her shoulders and closed her eyes.

After a few minutes in meditation, an amazing idea jumped out in her mind. The more she thought about it, the more excited she felt – so much so that she didn't want to open her eyes and risk spoiling her great idea and the wild imagination of her mind. By the time she opened her eyes, she had a clear plan that was so inspiring.

Her vision revolved around the children she had met earlier and the conversation with Liv, who reminded her that children don't forget anything if they are inspired and have a goal in front of them. Asking Liv to think about the next collection and teaching her how to use her creativity, she had created a goal for her to accomplish. *Children need us adults to guide and teach them how to achieve goals*, she thought. *I'm going to create a collection with homeless children or foster kids. They're our next generation; they need us the most and instead of guiding them, we ignore them. This is exactly what I'll do when I get back home. Together with The Delaney Brothers, we can create a great educational and inspirational platform for homeless children globally.*

She knew right away that she had the genesis of an unbelievable project. Instead of helping homeless children with food, which could only ever maintain survival on a daily basis, she could teach them how to use and develop creativity. It would be a great way for them to learn, grow and experience how a fashion collection is created.

"They can be the stars of the show from the beginning to the end of the project," she said aloud and the more she thought about it, the greater her excitement. Not wasting any time, she went to her desk and started to write all of her ideas down, maximising her plan. She was in such a zone of creativity and inspiration, she didn't even realise it had gone midnight…yet still she carried on writing in her journal.

Olivia didn't sleep much that night. She had a vision and didn't stop until she had everything on paper. It was like a mission that she had been given to accomplish. The next day, she had a lazy day by the beach…but her mind was in such a creative state, she started to create her master plan of how she could achieve and deliver her idea. Olivia was a natural dreamer who loved living in her imaginative world. This is how she created everything in her life, from her personal life to her great design creations; first, the formation of an idea in her mind, followed by the execution of it to make it become reality.

The next day, Olivia left the resort with Tom, having arranged to visit the orphanage housing, the children she had met on the beach. Telling him to drive to a shopping mall, she went to a stationary store and bought heaps of pens, pencils, drawing paper and everything else she needed, including plastic folders to keep their drawings clean and safe.

Finally arriving at a large house close to the beach, everybody there looked happy and welcoming. Olivia was introduced to a lady called Ead, who was the manager of the orphanage. She spoke a little English and was keen to find out why Olivia had paid them a visit. Olivia explained that she wanted to help and that the children there would be rewarded as a consequence. She went on to explain that she would talk to her employer about future funding, given it was supportive of child charities among others.

After a few minutes in her office, Olivia finally met the children, which delighted her. There were a few older ones, who helped the younger children but she felt sad at the way they had to live. Everything in the orphanage was very basic as it relied on charities and other funds to survive but her mission was to make those children smile and give them a purpose. Giving each child a folder with pencils, drawing paper, stickers and colouring books, she sat down with them and asked Tom to translate for her.

"I came here today to visit you all because I had a nice idea and believe you can help me accomplish it." Opening a folder for herself, she continued, "Do you like colouring and drawing?"

"Yes!" the children chorused loudly.

"Let me tell you a little story." She smiled. "As a child, I always dreamed and the best way to remember a dream and to express my feelings and inspirations was – and still is – in drawing and colouring. So, I maintain my creativity by keeping a record of it on paper and whenever I feel like I want to return to my dream, I perfect it on paper, so that it matches the images in my mind.

"I've seen a few of you drawing on the sand and, I must admit, I'm amazed at your talent. Don't be upset if you can't draw. Maybe you can colour better and some of you will have other talents. I'll tell you lots of other ways in which you can find and use your own creativity. To my knowledge, we're all creative but in different ways. Some of you might like numbers and create things with them. Some of you might like cooking and create a tasty dish from scratch. So ask yourself what you like or love the most, then start with that.

"Ead and her team will help and guide you. Remember, try your best to recreate your dream on paper and when I next

183

come to visit, we can sit down and talk about them and your little projects. Do you think you can do this?"

"Yes!" They all cried again excitedly, a number of hands shooting up in the air, keen to ask questions as if she was their teacher.

It was amazing for Olivia to see them excited and focused and, on the way back to the hotel, she felt such warm gratitude…a deep, internal happiness…the kind of feeling she only got when helping others and contributing to society.

The next day, Olivia packed her clothes and rearranged her travel. She knew that her friends wouldn't approve of her move but felt confident they would understand once she had given them an explanation. The thing was, Olivia couldn't stay any longer in Thailand. Her vision was driving her and she just knew that her work with the children was what she had been searching for in life. She always thought that when a person came into contact with something greater than themselves, it was so inspiring and pure it must become reality. *Our young generation needs our guidance and creativity*, she thought to herself. *It's what helps us to express and experiment with whatever we have in our minds. Especially homeless children, who need inspiration and guidance the most. If I can guide children with their development and teach them how to use their creativity, nothing in this world could be a better reward.*

Arriving back in the UK, she had barely put her case down at home before heading straight to the office. She wanted to share her great idea and inspiration with Sarah and was convinced that The Delaney Brothers would be happy to embark upon such a unique, special project with her. Making her way to Sarah's office, Olivia knocked on her door.

"Yes, come in!"

"Hi, Sarah!" Olivia greeted her with a huge smile.

"What are you doing here?" Sarah asked, standing with a look of surprise on her face.

"Aren't you supposed to be in Thailand?"

"Yes, I am." Grinned Olivia. "But a great vision and inspiration made me return. Please don't think I'm crazy but I just couldn't wait. In fact, once you hear it, you'll understand why." Sitting down on the sofa next to Sarah's desk, it took around 20 minutes for her to share her story and vision with Sarah.

"So, finally, my question is, what do you think of my idea to create a kids' collection with orphans or foster kids?"

Sarah looked enthused, explaining, "I really like the idea! We're doing so well with you in charge of the design department. Every decision you've made has worked 100 percent. Let me talk to Simon. If he feels the project is doable, we can add it to our portfolio and develop it. Then it would be yours to make it happen, thank you for sharing such a great idea with me!"

Olivia left the office with huge belief that her project would be green lit and with a week's holiday remaining, promised to use it to create a perfect business plan. But, for now, she needed to rest. Exhausted from travelling and sharing her vision with Sarah, she realised she had barely slept in over 24 hours, running on pure adrenaline. *I need to rest, then tomorrow I'll pick Duke up from the dog sitter and call Anna, Evelin and Andrew*, she thought.

The morning was a little cold and wet, Olivia dressing accordingly in trousers, chunky jumper and puffer jacket as she left to pick up Duke, her special, loving, loyal friend.

Frantic with joy at seeing her again, he jumped up and down upon seeing Olivia, who decided to take him straight to the park to have a nice run together before returning home. Watching him running and being so happy and playful, reminded her of the lovely children in Thailand.

The air was crisp and fresh and they spent a good hour in the park. It was a perfect way to start the day but her friends were on her mind and she was desperate to share with them her great new idea and adventure. Deep inside, she knew that no matter what, she would make it happen.

On the way home, she called Anna but to her surprise she didn't answer. Leaving her a short message, asking her to call her back, she then tried Evelin's number.

"Good morning, Evelin," she said when her friend answered.

"Hey! What time is it in Phuket? Lunch time?"

"Yes, in Phuket it's lunch time, but I'm back in England."

"Oh my God, what happened? Are you okay? Did you have some kind of medical emergency?"

"No, I'm fine. The truth is, I'm sorry to disappoint you all, but I had to come back. Why don't you come over today and we can talk about it? Or I can come to yours if that makes it easier."

"I'm out food shopping but I'll come by before I go home."

"Okay, sounds good," said Olivia. "Have you spoken to Anna and Andrew? I left a message on Anna's phone and was planning to call Andrew after I spoke to you."

"Are you sure there's nothing to worry about?" Evelin asked.

"Yes, everything's totally fine. I'm sorry to let you all down. I had to come back but I'll explain when you come over."

"Okay, see you shortly," said Evelin, ending the call.

Olivia was dialling Andrew's number when Anna called her back. "Hey, miss busy, are you okay?"

"Yes, I'm fine," answered Anna. "How are you and how's Phuket?"

"Phuket was beautiful but I'm back home now. Something important happened when I was there and I had to make a decision to stay or leave early."

"What could be more important than your health?" asked Anna. "Are you okay?"

"It's nothing to do with my health, Anna," said Olivia. "I need to see you to explain. I've just spoken to Evelin, who's on her way to my place. Come over but only if you can."

"Well, it's the weekend," said Anna, "so you're lucky – I can come by. Do you want a Starbucks coffee or a healthy smoothie?"

"A smoothie will be great, thank you."

"Well, see you shortly, strange woman. You've really intrigued me. Is Andrew coming as well? I know he's around today as I'm meeting him later."

"I haven't spoken to him since I got back but will call him now."

"Okay then, see you soon."

Calling Andrew directly afterwards, he seemed out of breath upon answering. "Hi, Miss Phuket, how are you today?"

"I'm well," said Olivia. "Are you running? It sure sounds like it."

"Yes! In fact, to make you a little homesick, I'm running in the park where you usually take Duke out."

"Sounds like I've just missed you, in that case."

"Are you serious? Don't tell me you're back home."

"Yes, I am. I need to apologise for not staying longer. I know you all made such a huge effort to arrange this great holiday for me. I feel bad but hope you'll all understand once I've had a chance to explain. Anna and Evelin are on their way to my place. Fancy joining us?"

"Absolutely," said Andrew. "As soon as I've finished my run. You're a strange little lady. I hope it's worth it but knowing you, it's probably more than worth it."

"Wait until you hear it!"

"Don't make me curious now! See you soon."

Olivia boiled a kettle of water and opened a packet of biscuits. She was a little nervous; after all, she owed them a proper explanation as to why she curtailed a holiday that her friends had put so much thought into. Once they all arrived, Olivia sat on the chair facing them and told them the story of how she came across Tom and how he introduced her to some great places, including the beach where she met the orphan children and baby elephant.

"It's interesting that you keep meeting orphan children, including little Olivia," said Anna.

"Yes, it is, and I know why…or at least I think I do," said Olivia. "While meditating, I had a vision that was so powerful, educational and inspirational. So, here it is – I want to help homeless children globally. I know it's a huge undertaking but I'll start with the UK first and then with a little help from The Delaney Brothers, I believe I can do it."

"Does the company know about it?" asked Evelin.

"Yesterday, when I arrived in the UK, I pretty much went straight to the office. I'm waiting to hear from Sarah, who promised to talk to Simon and let me know ASAP. I know it'll be fine – what company wouldn't want to contribute to one of the greatest educational global projects?"

"You might be surprised." Andrew cautioned. "Don't hold huge hopes for it. Big corporate companies don't take rational decisions like you, Olivia. They don't go with the heart; they go with a financial plan." He crossed his legs and sat back in his chair. "Don't get me wrong, this is an amazing idea and I love it. It's a great way to keep creativity going with the young generation, one of the most inspiring things I've ever heard. You're a genius! But not everybody will see or think the way you do."

"I agree, you're a born visionary," said Evelin, echoing Andrew's sentiments. "I admire your great mind and you always put other people before yourself. It takes an extraordinary person to do that, so I'm fully with you on this project."

"Well, I'm the black sheep of this friendship, but I must admit I like the idea," nodded Anna. "I agree with Andrew – it's genius. Who goes on holiday and comes back with an idea as big as this? Only Olivia, of course! Even on a holiday, she can't rest and be normal. I just love you so much! The only thing that makes me sceptical is that you're relying on The Delaney Brothers to create the project with you. I don't want you to be disappointed and make a huge mistake. You've created such an amazing career out of fashion and you're brilliant at it. That's my opinion, anyway."

"Well, let's see what happens," Olivia responded. "I think the company will see the advantages of it. It's a great business idea too if they want to look deeper from a financial perspective. We can attract lots of other companies, global artists, singers, architects, entrepreneurs, governing bodies and many more capable of investing and contributing. This is such a great humanitarian and educational project. It's not only about creativity in fashion – it's about creativity in general. Anything that exists in this world is because of our human creative mind."

Olivia knew she was a great speaker who expressed herself with passion while her knowledge and philosophical approach to everything touched many people. Her friends supported her and that mattered so much. She knew deep inside that this would be her life project and maintained her belief that The Delaney Brothers would welcome the idea and develop it with her.

She had a nice time with her friends and relied on their support and opinions. As soon as they left, she started to work on her business plan, wanting to have it ready by the time the company came back to her with an answer. Olivia had no fear of the unknown, driven purely by self-belief, excitement and what she thought was right. She loved sharing her thoughts with people and didn't mind criticism – to the contrary, she encouraged others to have their voice, to have no fear to express an opinion and to ensure that before anything was said, it had value, fairness and depth to it.

A few days passed by, then on the Tuesday afternoon she received an email from Simon and Sarah. Her heart was beating so hard and she had a nervous feeling before opening it. When she did, her face dropped. The email was nicely written but mainly focused on her recent job and how great she was doing while Simon very politely, but clearly, stated that the company couldn't take another project on board due to it focusing on international expansion in the Middle-East and Asia but that it was something that could be reviewed in the future.

Olivia couldn't believe that they had declined such a special project. *I'll send them a summary of the business plan that I've been working on*, she thought to herself. *Surely after looking at it, they'll clearly see what I can deliver. I'll take the responsibility to deliver the project within six months and they don't need to do much apart from saying yes.*

Olivia sat down and sent them a friendly email back. She added the facts, the figures and a compact business plan. She was still positive that once they saw it, they wouldn't be able to say no. She made clear that the project would be her responsibility and that, if after, say, six months, she failed, she would drop it. But by God, she did want The Delaney Brothers to put its weight behind it.

To her disappointment, she received an email back almost straight away. Instead of calling her to discuss the matter or to arrange a face-to-face meeting, Simon clearly stated that the company wasn't interested in any new projects at that moment in time. Her disappointment swelling, she read the conclusion of his email.

We are very happy to have you back at work from next week. I hope the holiday cleared your mind and helped you to rest. We have lots to do and I believe you have a great duty to focus on the design department. Since you left on holiday, it has stopped delivering its daily targets. The team needs you.

After reading the email several times, Olivia stood up from the sofa with a sad, disappointed look on her face. And then she felt angry – she had given so much to The Delaney Brothers, her time, her talent, her love…almost everything. She chose a career over love and had even ditched Damian for fear that she would have had to choose between the two. Yes, she had walked away from him because of his reaction to little Liv and, yes, her stubborn character and the alcohol she drank that night played their part but The Delaney Brothers had been on her mind too. She hadn't been ready for a radical change so soon into her time at the brand.

She had for several months been punishing herself with crazy amounts of work, almost bringing her health to the ground in the process. She had worked so hard – not that she had been forced but because she loved working – so how could Simon send an email and not even want to talk to her face to face? And as for reminding her of her duties…well, her duties were dictated by her ambitions in life and what she had to do to accomplish them.

Tempted to send a reply immediately, she resisted, not wanting it to come across in the wrong way and unable to ensure that some of her anger wouldn't be injected into her words. She looked at Duke and, stroking him, decided to take him out in the park, needing some fresh air and to relax. But still angry from the rejection by the time she returned home, she decided to sleep on it. Like Scarlett said in Gone with the Wind, *tomorrow is another day*.

Olivia kept her week busy with yoga classes, meditation and some other exercises. Then, on the Friday of that week, she sat down at her desk at home and decided to carefully think about and make a decision on what had happened earlier on that week. She didn't want to share her thoughts with her friends, knowing how they would react.

Her instinct was to resign from her job but she needed to ensure she wasn't making the decision based purely on the email she received. She chose instead to remember the nice memories of her time at The Delaney Brothers. The company had been great for her, welcoming her aboard and giving her lots of freedom in her role but that made perfect sense, given her great talent in design and entrepreneurial approach. But as much as she loved her work and her career with The Delaney Brothers, she had a bigger mission to accomplish – to guide and give hope to the young generation. The world needed people like her to have a voice and to express creativity in a different way.

Olivia picked a pen up and started to write her resignation letter. She wanted to send it by special courier, so that it would be delivered before the day ended. She had no guilt about leaving everything she had built over the last two years behind. Always trusting her instinct, her passion for her own project was so deeply rooted in her by now that she knew nothing would stop her achieving her goal.

To her surprise, The Delaney Brothers accepted her resignation with reluctance. So, to take her mind away from anything work-related, Olivia arranged to visit Liv at the weekend. She missed her loads and had a great idea that would see Liv help her with the project. Spending the entire evening writing and searching online, she found a few foster homes in the UK that she thought would welcome her plan.

The next day, with Duke by her side, she left early in the morning to visit little Olivia. Andrew calling her while she was driving.

193

"Hello, Andrew," she answered. "I'm driving, so you're on loud speaker."

"Okay, no problem. Where are you heading so early in the weekend? Oh, let me guess – visiting Liv."

"You know me too well! Yes, I am…and guess what? I have Duke with me too," said Olivia pulling over.

"I haven't heard from you this week. Usually, if it's bad news, I get the call and if it's a good one, I get it too. But this time I don't know what to think."

"I resigned yesterday," Olivia said without hesitation. "You were right – they didn't need any extra projects. I don't blame them. I understand. But I had to follow my instinct and vision. This project is exactly what I've been missing in my life."

"I knew that, the moment you told us," Andrew replied. "It's why you came back from your holiday early. It's a beautiful humanitarian project and you're the most caring, inspiring woman I know. I can only offer my help if you ever need it. You know I'm here for you."

Olivia felt quite emotional at Andrew's stance. He had decided to be there for her rather than focusing on the faults of her decision and understood that she was determined and strong and ready to progress with her project. "I appreciate that," she said. "Thank you. It means a lot."

"No problem. Be sure to give Liv a hug from me and let's get together over the weekend to brainstorm your life ambition."

"Okay, captain, try me on Sunday."

Arriving at little Liv's home, Olivia parked and let Duke out on a leash. She took a paper bag out of the car and headed towards the entry door but didn't even manage to press the doorbell when the door opened and Liv jumped into her arms, giving her and Duke a big hug. Olivia's face was so radiant and happy. Boy, had she missed this little girl…her little twin, who mirrored her not just in looks but personality too.

"Hello, my little friend!" She laughed, putting Liv down and handing her the paper bag. "This is something for you from Thailand."

Liv looked at her and with a huge smile said, "Thank you! I can't wait to see what's inside!"

"Do you want to go for a drive and maybe some brunch?" asked Olivia. "That way we can have a catch-up."

"It sounds like a great plan – yes, please!" Grinned Liv.

After a brief chat with Liv's foster parents, during which time she told them of her plans for the day, they left. While Olivia was driving, Liv looked in her goody bag and smiled with happiness. Out of the bag she pulled a statuette of an elephant, some pretty stationary and a card.

"You're the best!" Liv declared. "Thank you for all of these lovely presents. Are there lots of elephants in Thailand?"

"Yes, lots. Elephants are Thailand's national symbol. The one that you have is called the white elephant, is a symbol of royalty in Thailand. The people in Thailand celebrate their longevity, strength and durability. While in Phuket, I met a group of children on the beach and they were playing with a baby elephant. That was a great experience!"

She didn't know whether to mention that the children were orphans but knowing how sensitive and bighearted Liv was, decided against it. She would tell her one day but Liv deserved to be happy and to forget that she was a foster child.

Liv cuddled the elephant and said, "I have a name for my elephant. Would you like to know what it is?"

"Yes – tell me!"

"It's Angel, the elephant!" she said enthusiastically.

"What a nice name!" Olivia smiled. "Hello, Angel, the elephant! From now on, you'll have a nice mummy called Olivia, who'll protect you and look after you."

"Yes," said Liv with a huge smile on her face.

Finding a nice local café, Olivia ordered food and drinks, then spoke to Liv. "I have a proposal for you and hope you'll accept it. Of course, your foster guardians will have to confirm that you're allowed to be a part of it and we'll have to get the approval of your school too. So, here it is…are you ready?"

"Yes," shrieked an excited Liv.

"I have a great plan and a new project and I'd like you to help me with it. I left my job this week because I believe so much in this, a super special children's collection that I want to create with you and a lovely group of kids.

"You can be my right-hand girl and muse. I think it's a great opportunity for us to teach and inspire creativity in other children. I specifically thought of foster children and I want to know what you think. I chose foster children because they need more guidance, love, help, inspiration and attention. Creating a collection with kids will be educational and a great opportunity to give a chance to create something unique. To make them little heroes and let them enjoy the moment."

Liv was so excited; she kept jumping up and down in her seat. "I love it! When will we start to work on it together? I have lots of drawings and made an inspirational board – you

196

need to see it! You taught me how to draw and how to think about the design, the colour and what's popular."

"I'm so proud of you – you remember everything! That's why I need you to help me. Can you imagine? We can teach other children how to create and develop a collection and you'll learn so much more along the way too."

After eating brunch, the girls headed back to Liv's place. They reached her home and the little one ran out of the car and straight in through the door, her parents opened for her, having heard Olivia pulling up. Running upstairs into her room, she grabbed the drawing book and colourful board she had made. Olivia was talking to her foster parents when Liv ran back downstairs.

"Is everything okay?" Liv asked in a soft, girly voice.

"Yes, of course," said Olivia. "Because you'll be helping me with my project!"

"Yes!" screamed little Liv. "I'm going to be a designer!" Bursting into dance, her eyes were so alive, her smile contagious. Liv handed Olivia the drawings and inspiration board. "I hope you like them – I'm so excited!"

Olivia looked at the board and drawings. It was clear to her that the little one already had great talent. Her drawings were so beautiful and the board was very well thought through. "Have you done all of these on your own?"

"Yes!" Liv nodded enthusiastically.

"This is amazing – I love them all and am sure we can use some of them in the project! Would you like that?"

"Yes!" Liv cried loudly.

Olivia had happy tears running down her face and believed even more strongly that her decision to resign and follow her instinct was 100 percent the right one. *Ask a child to help create something and the results are just so rewarding. An innocent smile and joy are the best things we can experience as humans*, she thought.

"I'll see you next week," she said, giving Liv a big hug, the pair high-fiving.

Chapter Nine
Like Life, Fashion Has No Limits – If There Isn't a Way, Then You Must Create One

Six months later and everything had changed. Olivia obtained support from the government and the fashion council and had designers volunteering to help with the project! And, of course, her friends had been there for her from day one. That's not to say that everything was as easy as it looked but her strong will and passion for her amazing vision brought a few foster agencies, children's foundations and many more organisations together, which were happy to work with her and help her achieve her objectives.

A few young designers, Liv and herself, had managed to teach and guide 40 children how to create a fashion collection from scratch. As for the children's education, Olivia ensured they wouldn't miss out, arranging a special school programme for a few months before they took their summer holidays, during which they spent the majority of their time learning and creating the project together. And since they had only just returned to school for the winter term, she had arranged a hybrid educational programme that enabled them to see the project through to fruition.

Olivia was in a large room, looking like a proper fashion atelier, surrounded by lots of children and a few more adults. She sat down in a corner of the room and closed her eyes for a minute. A flashback sequence started to play out in her mind, reminding her of both happy and sad times. She saw the first day of her project, being driven to different foster houses and picking the little ones up and being in the bus that drove them, the kids being loud and happy, one minute singing and another arguing…though Olivia smirked at their innocence.

Sitting just behind the driver, she kept looking back at them and smiling. And when they arrived at the atelier, the children ran inside the building, looking everywhere and checking the place out.

"Is this where we'll come every day to study?" asked one boy, called Thomas.

"Yes, it is," said Olivia. "Do you like it?"

"Yes, it's very nice! If you need any extra help, just let me know," he responded, gazing into Olivia's eyes.

"Yes, of course – I shall keep that in mind. Thank you for offering." She smiled. Turning to the other children, she asked, "Please, find a place to sit down and I'll introduce you to your teachers. You've already met Liv, of course. Now please meet Laura, Victoria and Liam."

Introducing the children to the designers, it was a breath of fresh air, seeing them so passionate and full of inspiration. On that day, they came up with the name of the collection and its main inspirational colour. Liv stood up and told them the story of how she met Olivia and how she kept thinking about her every night. Then, to Olivia's surprise, all of the children wanted to tell a little story that they had dreamed about. It was very emotional because Olivia and her team wanted to help them achieve their dreams. Those dreams represented another challenge, which she hoped would come true but for now they had to focus on the project.

"We all have nice stories," one of the girls, Etti, suggested. "So why don't we make one together?"

Olivia smiled and said, "That's exactly why we're here today. We'll create a great story together and my hope is to inspire children around the globe to join what we're starting today, so that we can learn and create memories together."

Talking with the children and letting them express themselves was so inspiring. Liv and Kai, a very academic boy, who loved science, started to debate what they should call the collection.

"I really like something like magic," said Liv.

Kai stood up and said, "I think legacy might be better."

Such a big, meaningful word for a little boy aged thirteen, thought Olivia.

Most of the children liked magic, while others went with Kai and Legacy.

Olivia looked at them and said, "Why don't we keep both names and call it The Magic Legacy?"

As if in one voice, the children screamed, "Yes, that's a cool name!"

That exact moment represented the crystallisation of their happy, creative journey together. Olivia wanted the collection to be all about their thoughts and vision and was taken back in time by a flashback that reminded her of an interview she gave to a magazine. The journalist completely reinvented the story of her vision, making it look more like child slavery. It was so painful and detrimental to her and she had since refused to accept any interview requests to keep her focused on her mission.

That interview almost ruined her reputation but she didn't give up. To her surprise, most of the nation's papers and magazines gave her their support, writing inspirational columns and articles. Olivia, as always, remained positive and continued her journey. She attracted lots of international press too and was kind and polite to everybody but refused to give them anything other than the main thrust of the project.

"You'll have to attend our first fashion show," she said in a statement. "This'll be the first time I'll speak publicly about the story and vision behind the project."

Following her heart and focusing on what really mattered was so important to Olivia, as was achieving something that had never been done before, which required huge dedication. Pursuing the project was pure pleasure, challenges were fuel for her adrenaline and impossible was a word that she refused to accept…in fact, as she often reminded people, the word itself meant I'm possible.

The voice of a child brought her back to reality.

"Miss Olivia!" a boy kept saying. "Can you hear me?"

"Yes, of course, I can hear you, Thomas," she said, looking at him. "Sorry, I drifted off somewhere."

"That's okay, I do that all the time." Smiled Thomas. "The samples are ready. We've been waiting for you."

Just 11 years old, he spoke like an adult and was one of the 40 foster kids who had been involved in creating the collection. He became Olivia's little manager and had such a strong, serious appearance and character. The dedication and abundance of creativity that these children had, was beyond magical. Their passion for the collection was so pure and inspiring, especially as it had assumed a far bigger dimension than she could have imagined.

It was only two days before the big day that everybody had been waiting for…just two days before the most anticipated fashion show in the world and Olivia kept her word not to divulge anything more about the origins of the project, concentrating on allowing the children to focus on the build-up to the event, the enjoyment from which would be their true reward.

Olivia followed Thomas into the middle of the room, where lots of the children were gathered, needing to practice rehearsals for the big day. The samples were finalised, so all that remained to do was structure and practice the catwalk to ensure that they included everything they wanted in the show. Olivia had filmed the entire journey since its genesis, a group of students lending her their assistance. She wanted to create a short video and start the show with that and wanted it to speak for itself and show the entire public what they had achieved, and how.

"Hello, my champions!" Olivia greeted the children. "The Magic Legacy collection is ready, all we have left to do now is make sure our rehearsals for the catwalk are organised and the rest of the details are in place and ready for the show. We've done so much since we started almost seven months ago. I'm so proud of you all. You showed me what discipline, passion, love, determination, talent, inspiration and, most of all, creativity means from your imagination.

"I hope and know that you'll continue with this work after the show. You can all teach and inspire other children with the skills you've learned in this short, yet very intense, time.

Next door, we have a large room ready for us, for the rehearsals. I know you're very curious where the show will take place but I want you all to have the greatest surprise tomorrow. All I can say is that it's a very special place and I guarantee you'll love it."

Making their way next door, the room was empty with a two-metre-wide carpet stretching from one side of the room to the other.

"Do you know why the carpet is there?" Laura asked the other children.

"It's the catwalk path!" most of them said in response.

"That's exactly right! Now I'd like you to help me please. Can any of you show me what a catwalk looks like when it's being used?"

"I can!" shouted another of the children.

"Great, come over, Yasmin and show us how you walk the catwalk."

Yasmin courageously walked over to the beginning of the carpet and, adopting a rather serious look, started to walk. She really knew how to carry it off – she had her hips and legs moving like a pro. Everybody clapped and smiled.

"Yasmin, that was very impressive," said Laura. "I think you can be in charge of helping your friends here do the same. Let's create four groups of ten children. This way, it'll be much better to learn."

After several hours of rehearsals, the children all sat down on the floor. Bringing some snacks for them, Liam and Victoria helped to fairly divide them. Then, the next day, they continued with the rehearsals, after which Olivia showed the children the video that would open the show. Lasting five minutes, it showed in great detail how the children did their research, created the inspirational board, came up with the designs, did the drawings, chose which designs went forward as samples and even helped with some of the basic sewing. The kids were so happy to see themselves on the screen and couldn't believe they would be on television.

"You've done all of this great work and I'm so proud of you all," Olivia told them. "We only taught and guided you – you did the rest. Are you happy with what you've learned on our journey together and what you've achieved?"

"Yes – we're very happy!" they shouted in unison.

"Thank you for giving us such an opportunity," said Thomas. "We can't wait for the fashion show tomorrow – it's so exciting," he continued with a huge smile on his face.

All of them giggled, confirming their excitement and went to give Olivia and the other designers big hugs. They reviewed the whole show from the beginning to the end. By then, Laura reminded Olivia that it was 5 pm – goodness, how quickly the day had gone.

Surprised, Olivia looked at everybody and said, "We have to go home and have a nice early night. We have a great day awaiting us tomorrow. Come on, let's wrap everything up and go home. We did more than we expected today."

After dropping everybody back to their respective homes, Olivia asked Liv's foster parents to let her have a sleepover. Agreeing to her request, Olivia drove back home, Liv falling asleep in the car. Unable to answer Evelin's call, she made it back home and parked in her driveway, gently carrying Liv into the house and marvelling at how sweet she looked when laying her down in a spare room.

Heading back downstairs to the living room, Olivia called Evelin. She was tired but so happy and fulfilled.

"Oh, hi, Olivia. How's the little one?" asked Evelin.

"Oh, she's fine. Actually, she's upstairs in the land of nod. Her foster parents said she could have a sleepover." Zapping her car shut, she closed the front door. "I'm so excited about tomorrow! What an amazing journey I've had with that little angel Liv and the rest of the children. I'm so blessed and grateful. Even if I had words to describe my feelings, they still wouldn't justify how I feel right now. Life is the most beautiful journey we have – we just need to find our purpose. I'm so lucky to have found mine and to help change the lives of these amazing children forever."

"You're absolutely right," Evelin responded. "I must admit, I'm very curious and can't wait for tomorrow as well. I almost feel like a child! You've achieved something so unique and powerful."

"Thanks to you all," said Olivia. "Your great support and help have been so important to me. I'm looking forward to seeing you all tomorrow. Are you coming all together or separately?"

"Andrew's coming with Anna and I'm coming with David and Francis. We'll be there to support you and to help if you need us."

"Oh, yes," Olivia said enthusiastically. "Tomorrow will be the best day of my life…a day that'll be remembered, cherished and used as an example for my future aspirations. Inspiring creativity and contributing to the education of our young generation is my life path."

"That all sounds great," said Evelin. "I'd better go now, so night-night. I love and admire you."

"Love you too – night-night."

Olivia went to bed very late, unable to calm her overactive mind. Next morning, when her alarm woke her, she opened her eyes and stretched under the bed linen smiling. After some meditation and a short yoga session, she went downstairs and started preparing breakfast when Liv entered the kitchen, giving her a hug.

"Did you sleep well, my fashionista friend?" Olivia asked smiling.

"Like a baby," replied Liv, sitting at the kitchen table ready for breakfast.

Liv had funny expressions and Olivia loved her sense of humour. They had a very busy, exciting day ahead. Olivia's discipline helped her stay on top of all that she did and, being such a great organiser, she had everything under control. Making a few phone calls, she double checked if everything was progressing as it should have been, then headed into London with Liv.

The atelier was situated in Chelsea and the mystery venue wasn't far from there. On the way into London, Liv asked Olivia something.

"I know the venue's a surprise but I think you can tell me now. I promise I won't tell anybody," she said looking at Olivia with her innocent eyes.

"I know you won't say anything but I think you deserve a surprise too. And I just know you'll love the venue."

"Ah, you're teasing me!"

Arriving at the atelier, Olivia asked one of her colleagues to keep an eye on Liv, then headed straight to the surprise venue – the Natural History Museum. Olivia was so grateful when South Kensington council, offered her the use of the museum for the fashion show. Being such a humanitarian project, Olivia had fantastic support and help from the government – and even the Royal family, which had brought her tears of joy.

The building itself was an integral part of British heritage and its architecture so unique and powerful. Olivia kept it as a surprise for the children, knowing how excited they would be about the specimens therein and its history. She had arranged a private tour for all of them a few hours before the show to see what was there and understand the history of such a magnificent place. She wanted all of the children to have an unforgettable fairy tale experience…a day that would shape their lives forever.

Entering the museum, she was so happy, seeing almost everything for the show already in place. The podium was built and all of the preparations were under control. Everything looked exactly as she expected and, hearing Andrew's voice, she turned to face him smiling.

"So, what do you think?" she asked as Andrew kissed her on the cheek.

"I'm beyond happy with your organising skills – you've done a terrific job, so thank you. This afternoon, this very special place will hold a great show that'll inspire and help our society, bringing the best out of our young generation…and all thanks to you and your great mind! The guide is ready when the children arrive and I've organised a few volunteers to dress up in animal costumes to welcome them."

"You're a genius," said Olivia as another voice interrupted their conversation.

"Olivia, the children are on their way," said Laura. "Do you want to go over everything before they arrive?"

"Yes, please – that's a must. Let's go," said Olivia, leaving with Laura.

Looking at the rails, the nicely organised capsules and shoes positioned under every outfit, Olivia saw that each piece of clothing had a child's picture on it to make it easier when the show started. Every detail that Olivia and her team had planned for had been successfully integrated into the forthcoming show. All they had to do now was wait for the big moment.

"Laura, I'm so grateful to you and the rest of the team. This has been a special journey for all of us and, I must admit, I feel like I'm living in a dream at the moment."

Laura heard on her walkie-talkie that the children had arrived. She and Olivia went outside to see the bus stop in front of the venue. Screaming with joy, the people in the costumes helped them off the bus, giving them a little present; a Natural History Museum badge.

"Here," said Olivia, handing Laura a microphone with which to address the children. "Tell them about the private tour."

Little Liv ran to Olivia with tears in her eyes. "This is amazing," she said. "You're the best at surprises!"

Before Olivia had a chance to react, Laura started to speak to the children.

"I've been asked to announce a great surprise for you all. So, here goes, you're going to have a private tour of the museum! This way, you can see all of the animals and almost everything that the museum has. So…are you ready?"

The children could barely contain themselves screaming with excitement. After two hours of touring the museum, learning some facts and history, they had their last rehearsal for the catwalk. With the show fast approaching, final preparations were made backstage and the road outside was temporarily closed with press from across the globe, anxiously awaiting the show. Olivia had arranged for a big cinema screen to be attached to the side of the museum, so that the people outside could watch it live.

She rushed to get ready and, once her makeup and hair had been done, she rushed to put her dress on. Not long after, it was time for the show to finally begin. Olivia looked at the children, sitting in a long line, waiting to make their way onto the catwalk. The short video that she made started to play amid dead silence, other than the voices of those featuring in it.

It was easy to see the emotional, positive effect the video had on those watching and, when it ended, the entire audience, both within the venue and outside, erupted with huge applause and cheering. Beautiful, angelic music started to play, a huge light from the ceiling brightened the whole room and that's when it was possible to see the theme of the show with white the dominant colour. A huge white flower featured on the central wall while the podium was bedecked with them. The whole place was like heaven on earth.

When the music slowed down, little Liv opened the show dressed in a beautiful princess white dress with a little blue detail on the belt and shoes. She looked like an angel and everybody was mesmerised by her courage and confidence as she strutted down the catwalk. Reaching the end of the podium, where a huge staircase was placed, she walked up a few steps and turned to the audience, made a heart out of her hands and sent it to them.

At that moment the children, one by one, started to enter the show. It was so magical that the audience fell under a great spell. All 40 children walked on the podium, one after the other. They all wore predominantly white clothes with each design having an accent pertaining to their favourite colour. The girls mainly wore skirts, blouses and dresses, while some boys were wearing casual white trousers with colour details on them and T-shirts adorned with electric, colourful words and pictures.

Other boys wore classic white chinos with shirts, again having accent colours on them – an idea that the children came up with. White represented the light, innocence and purity while the electric colours included red, yellow, green, orange, pink, blue, black and purple. The other children went on the stairs next to Liv and made heart shapes with their hands. Love was the message they wanted to share…and the show captured the heart of every single spectator.

Olivia took to the stage with a huge smile, wearing a stunning white sleeveless dress. It was a Greek/Roman style gown with a satin electric blue fin belt that was wrapped around her high waist several times over. Olivia looked so beautiful and powerful like an Athenian Goddess! But her ostensible confidence masked a nervousness and every part of her body shook with happiness.

As she looked at the end of the podium, the children were waving at her. For a few seconds, her eyes were fixated on the grand room with the staircase. It was only then that she realised she was enacting a dream she had a few years ago, which had featured the staircase and the white dress she was wearing. She felt so empowered and confident, telling herself, "That's how dreams come true!"

Olivia waved at the children and asked them to stand next to her. She opened her arms and they all ran to her, hugging her. Liv handed her the microphone and, looking out at the audience, Olivia said, "I'm blown away by your warmth, positivity and support. Thank you simply can't justify my feelings right now. I do, however, have a little message for you all but before I do that, I'd love to invite to the stage my team, which has been working with me for the last seven months. Thanks to their knowledge, patience and guidance, our little ones have experienced an unbelievable creative journey.

"I'm very grateful for all of the support, help and kind donations that we've received, including from our great government, local council, close friends, corporate companies, banks and many more. Without you all, this great project would never have happened. Thank you for believing in me and my great team."

The whole team filled the podium up and everybody stood up and cheered for them, including Olivia. She kept saying thank you to her amazing team and clapping them. After a minute or so of cheering and applause, Olivia addressed the audience again.

"I'd like to sincerely thank all of our little champions. The collection that they created and named The Magic Legacy will be the first collection that gave birth to a powerful new brand that I'm proudly calling Legacy. It'll be a charity foundation that provides homeless and foster children clothes and resources. But not only that, 20 percent of all income generated will go to different child foundations to help grow and develop creativity and education globally."

Looking again at the audience, she spotted her friends Andrew, Anna, Evelin, David and Francis holding hands together and looking at her with pride.

"My message to you all is simple," she continued. "Curiosity, determination, resilience and persistence helps us find the key to our purpose in life. To me, the fundamental and noblest art in life is to contribute and make a difference. Dreams do become reality; we just need the courage to believe in them. What drives our young generation in fashion is the beauty and magic of the creative world...the glamour, illusion and imagination. If together we guide them and give them a chance, the results can only be an abundance of love, success, happiness and satisfaction."

At that moment, looking far into the audience near the exit, Olivia locked eyes with Damian. She could have sworn that her heart stopped beating. Although she was nervous and emotional, she continued her address, "I sincerely hope that what we've experienced today will continue growing. I hope it will inspire other creatives from different backgrounds – artists, performers, architects and many more – to join us and ensure the Legacy brand lives forever. Together, we can create, inspire and make a difference in human education and our young generation."